WHAT HAPPENED TO HAMMOND?

How could a dead body travel sixty miles almost instantaneously through a bitter winter's night? Chief Inspector Garth could deal with three-dimensional problems, but Hammond's inexplicable transition was beyond him. Garth called in Dr. Carruthers to see if the eminent physicist could explain the mystery. The Doctor could! But not until a further baffling murder had been committed could Carruthers demonstrate — by means of a strangely airborne teapot — exactly what happened to Hammond.

JOHN RUSSELL FEARN

WHAT HAPPENED TO HAMMOND?

Complete and Unabridged

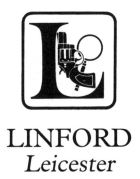

LINFORD
Leicester

First published in Great Britain

First Linford Edition
published 2006

British Library CIP Data

Fearn, John Russell, *1908 – 1960*
    What happened to Hammond?.
    —Large print ed.—
    Linford mystery library
    1. Police—England—Fiction
    2. Murder—Investigation—England—Fiction
    3. Detective and mystery stories
    4. Large type books
    I. Title
    823.9'12 [F]

    ISBN 1–84617–569–0

Published by
F. A. Thorpe (Publishing)
Anstey, Leicestershire

Set by Words & Graphics Ltd.
Anstey, Leicestershire
Printed and bound in Great Britain by
T. J. International Ltd., Padstow, Cornwall

This book is printed on acid-free paper

1

The message comprised three words — *Any Moment Now!* Each word was cut from a newspaper and pasted on to cheap yellow notepaper.

Benson T. Hammond read the three words in their different sizes of type, then crushed the trashy yellow envelope in his palm. He threw the envelope in the waste bin beside his desk and snapped on the desk-phone.

'Miss Barrow, come here a moment.'

Bethinking himself, Hammond retrieved the envelope from the bin and flattened it out on the desk. He performed the task with an almost feminine gentleness — and with good reason. All his life he had been forced to take exquisite care of himself. A disease — *fragilitas ossium-tarda* — made his bones as brittle as glass.

Miss Barrow, his personal secretary, came into the office. She was tall, long-nosed, with grey eyes and a school-marm hairdo.

'Good morning, Mr. Hammond,' she greeted. 'I — '

'I said 'good morning' when I entered the office,' Hammond interrupted. 'I want some information, Miss Barrow. Where did you find this letter?'

'In the mail box with the others. Unstamped and marked 'Personal', as you can see. There have been three similar letters, sir, all in the same vulgar-looking envelopes. And all of them unstamped and marked 'Personal'. You must have noticed — '

'Yes — and so have you, apparently.' Hammond raised a hand. 'I'm not blaming you. So, somebody pushed this letter — and the three preceding letters — through the mailbox during the night. For the life of me I can't think how, with a night watchman on guard.'

'Unless he was asleep,' Miss Barrow said coldly.

'Mmmm — possible. Obviously the reason for the delivery by hand is to prevent a postmark being shown.'

Hammond got to his feet — a shortish, broad-shouldered man bordering on sixty. His florid face and clear blue eyes, together with the short-cropped gray hair, gave him every appearance of strength. Strength he had — except for his peculiar bone structure.

'Miss Barrow, I'm being threatened,' he said, gazing out of the office window on to the busy shipping yards. His eyes lifted to a gigantic sign in the distance, which said — *Hammond (London Limited) Freight Shipping Line*.

'Threatened with what, sir?' Miss Barrow asked.

Hammond sat down again at the desk and handed her the note. She read it without a trace of expression, then returned the note to the desk.

'What are you going to do about it, sir?'

'Inform the police. Each of these notes has become a little more threatening. Up to now I have treated the whole thing as a joke, but this idiot actually sounds as though he means business.'

Hammond got up suddenly. He went over to the stand and took down his

Homburg and overcoat. Miss Barrow held his coat as he struggled into it.

'I'll be back shortly,' he said. I'm going to see Inspector Garth at the Yard. He's a good friend of mine. Maybe he'll have some suggestions to make.'

Miss Barrow nodded and watched as her employer put the note and envelope in his wallet, then she held the office door open for him. She smiled reflectively to herself as she returned to her own sanctum. It was a pleasure to her to see the tight-fisted, ruthless shipping tycoon scared for once in his life.

★ ★ ★

Chief Inspector Mortimer Garth looked up without surprise from his desk in the murky office overlooking the Thames embankment when Detective-sergeant Whittaker opened the door to Hammond. The shipper had already been announced over the phone.

'Well, Hammond — glad to see you!' Garth got to his feet. His death mask expression gave place to a smile.

''Morning, Garth.' Hammond held out his hand and then withdrew it again. 'Wait a minute!' he ordered. 'I've just remembered your strong handgrip. Take it easy — '

'I never knew a chap so chary of shaking hands,' Garth commented. 'What's the matter? Rheumatism?' He motioned to a chair. 'Have a seat. Hell, What with my indigestion, we're a pair of has-beens! Oh, you've met Detective-sergeant Whittaker before, I think?'

'How are you, sir?' Whittaker acknowledged, a youngish square-faced man with a beefy neck.

Hammond nodded impatiently. 'Sit down, Garth; I need to talk to you — professionally. I think my life's in danger! Take a look at this.'

Garth took the crumpled envelope and note and considered them. 'Kid's stuff,' he said finally.

'Not with three other notes like this in precedence!' Hammond snapped. 'Four notes altogether, each one couched in stronger terms. And now this one. 'Any moment now'. It's beyond a joke, Garth.'

'But what is supposed to happen at any moment?'

'None of the notes has said, but it can't be anything pleasant. I want police protection: I'm important enough to the community and commerce to have it.'

'Three others, you say? Where are they?'

'I destroyed them, thinking they were a joke. Now I realize the matter is serious.'

Garth shook his head. 'As head of a big freight shipping line, you must have enemies — but any serious enemy wouldn't resort to this kind of schoolboy rubbish. They wouldn't send advance warning of what they intend to do. And in any case there seems nothing in these notes to suggest anything terrible is going to happen — they don't even fall under the heading of threatening letters or intimidation.'

'Well, I don't like it,' Hammond snapped. 'All the notes were pushed in the general mail box at night, somehow eluding the night watchman, and had no postmark on the envelopes.'

Garth grinned. 'That wouldn't stop us

finding the culprit if we really had to, believe me. But this is hardly a job for our department. Somebody is just trying to make you uncomfortable.'

'You mean that I don't get any protection? That I can go about my business never knowing but what somebody will try and finish me?'

'What's really worrying you?' Garth asked bluntly. 'Surely a man of your character isn't scared to death by a few childish notes?'

Hammond said: 'It's not death that I'm afraid of — not the sudden bullet or the knife in the dark — but the lingering threat. I'm scared of being hit or beaten up or knocked about in any way. It would finish me . . . '

Garth looked his puzzlement.

'I suffer from *fragilitas ossiumtarda*. My physician can verify that. That's why I like to go easy on the handshakes.'

'Mmmm. Isn't that something to do with the bones?'

'It means an abnormal brittleness of bone. I'm a walking glass ornament. For most of my childhood I lay in bed. It was sheer hell. At maturity I gained a certain strength and could get about. I did. I built up my business. I married. I have a daughter . . . But, if a series of blows were to hit me now and because of them I landed back in bed for the rest of my life I'd die. It'd kill me. I couldn't stand it again.'

'Well, that's different,' Garth said. He stood up and held out his hand gingerly. 'I'll see that you at least get protection, Hammond, but I'll have a word with the A.C. first. Your strange complaint and standing in the community ought to entitle you to a couple of plainclothes men to keep watch over you — at least until the notes stop. In the meantime I'll see what can be done about tracing the sender of them.'

Hammond stood up, relief flooding his florid features. 'I knew I could count on you, Garth,' he said.

⋆ ⋆ ⋆

A young man loomed out of the November drizzle and knocked heavily on the door of Benson T. Hammond's Maida Vale residence. The door opened and amber light scythed across the early evening gloom.

'Oh, Mr. Dell,' the butler greeted, pleasantly. 'Good evening, sir. Miss Hammond is expecting you. She is in the lounge.'

'Good evening, Hilton. Rotten night.'

Harvey Dell stepped into the hall and took off his hat and mackintosh. He was a medium-sized, power-packed young man with black hair and blue eyes. He had the physique of an athlete and the face of a thinker. The largeness of his mouth and the abrupt stop at the end of his nose precluded claims to good looks — but he had a ready smile and amiability that had won him far more friends than enemies.

Hilton crossed the wide hall and opened a door. Before he could make an announcement a girl came hurrying out.

'Harvey!' He found himself suddenly gripped by the girl's clinging arms. 'It's so good to see you again! Come and sit down in this chair by the fire.'

The girl led him to an easy chair

evidently placed in readiness. She settled opposite him, half coiled on an enormous hassock. Her features were familiar to Harvey: a delicate mouth, rather long nose, a mass of copper-gold hair, and inquiring grey-blue eyes.

'This,' Harvey said awkwardly, 'is the night, Claire!'

She nodded vigorously. 'Dad came in fairly early tonight. He's in his study now, and he'll be there for the next half hour until it's time for him to change for dinner.'

Harvey laughed nervously. 'All day whilst I've been at work in the lab, I've been rehearsing my speech to your father. Yet now I'm here I can't seem to remember a single statement.'

'You don't need to!' Claire exclaimed. 'All you have to do is ask him if he's any objections to our becoming engaged. He *can't* have,' she went on, dismissing such a possibility. 'After all, it's only deference which makes you ask him at all. We are at an age to please ourselves. And you've a remarkably good social background, and you've a good position with the Noonhill

Teleradio Combine —What more is wanted?'

'Might want a lot more, Claire. You forget that you are the daughter of an extremely wealthy man and I'm nowhere near his class.'

'That doesn't signify. When Dad was your age he hadn't as much as you've got now.' Claire got to her feet, a small, even ethereal girl, very much like the mother who had died when she had been born. 'Time to take the plunge,' she said. 'Come on!'

Claire had told Harvey to come tonight since Monday was her father's quietest day at the office, and he would be in a good humour. However, Claire did not know about the disturbing threats and, Scotland Yard notwithstanding, his mood was not of the happiest.

The couple went down the broad hall, arm-in-arm. Reaching the study door at the far end of the hall the girl paused, then rapped once.

'Yes, come in,' her father's voice invited.

Harvey felt a shove in the small of his back. As he entered the room he had a painted smile and a great deal of assumed

11

dignity. The door closed again.

Outside, Claire was tempted to listen at the door. But when it came to temptation Claire Hammond had certain principles. Finally she went to the staircase and sat down on the third step.

'No, I won't hear of it!' The words came faintly and from a distance, in the unmistakable voice of Benson T. Hammond. The voice dropped again to inaudible muttering — then it changed slightly as Harvey spoke sharply. The words were blurred . . .

Bang! Like a desk being thumped. Harvey's voice was suddenly clear and insistent.

' . . . chance to beat the airlines at their own game, if you weren't so hide-bound . . . '

Claire relaxed. So they were not arguing about the engagement after all, but business. 'Damned rubbish, young man!' declared the shipper, still speaking in his most inflexible key.

' . . . and the cuts in shipping rates . . . distances are bound to be . . . You *must* . . . '

Muttering. Words with no sense, like men talking in their sleep. Then the study door was snatched open and Claire rose swiftly from her perch at the bottom of the stairs.

'Wasting my time like this!' her father exclaimed angrily. 'Hilton will show you out, Harvey — and you can stay out too as far as I'm concerned.'

'All right, I will!' Harvey retorted, and came striding down the hall as the study door slammed to again. He paused as Claire flitted forward.

'Harvey — Dearest!' She caught his arm tightly. 'What's happened? Wouldn't he — ?'

'He did at first and then changed his mind!' Harvey was breathing hard. 'He's nothing but a — '

The study door opened again sharply. 'I thought I told you to leave, Harvey,' Hammond said.

Harvey compressed his lips and glanced up as Hilton came pacing into view, summoned by Hammond ringing from the study.

'Hilton, Mr. Dell is leaving! Kindly see

that he does so immediately.'

'Very good, sir.'

'But *Harvey* — !' Claire had tears in her grey-blue eyes.

'I'll write you,' he whispered. 'And I'll explain everything. Now I'd better go.'

He withdrew from her grasp, grabbed his hat and mackintosh and then departed without a backward glance. Outraged, Claire swung round to where her father was still standing in the study doorway.

'What did you say to him?' she demanded, her eyes flaming.

Her father motioned her into the study and closed the door. 'You don't have to let the whole household hear, do you?' he asked.

'I don't care who hears — '

'*Sit down!*'

Hammond motioned to a chair opposite his desk, and such was the authority in his voice the girl obeyed. 'Dad, why did you have to *do* it?' she implored. 'Don't you realize that I love and want to marry him? You haven't raised any objections to our seeing each other — so why bring the axe down now?'

'If you only knew it, Claire, I've saved you from a fortune-hunter,' Hammond said. 'That is all Harvey Dell is.'

'Harvey's nothing of the sort,' Claire retorted. 'He's a — '

'I admit,' Hammond interrupted, 'that I never suspected it until tonight. But when a young man comes in here and first asks me for my daughter's hand, and then asks me for a cool two million pounds to finance an idea of his, what am I supposed to think?'

'Harvey did that?' Claire asked in amazement. 'Two million pounds?'

'Exactly! As soon as I'd consented to your engagement, he plunged into his request for money. Some high-flown notion he's got. The man's crazy!' Hammond's eyes narrowed. 'Give him two million and both you and he and the money would promptly vanish to foreign climes. I know his sort . . . He can't play the fool with me, Claire. I retracted my consent to the engagement and told him to get out.'

'But Dad, I — I can't *understand* it!'

Claire insisted. 'He never mentioned anything about money to me ... He always seemed to have plenty.'

'Maybe — but two million is more than plenty.' Hammond smiled grimly. 'Fortune-hunting young men of his calibre always keep the girl in the case in the dark and try and bamboozle the father. But no daughter of mine is going to have anything to do with him!'

Claire was silent, her romantic hopes blasted sky-high.

'It's for your own good, Claire,' Hammond went on. 'You are not to see Harvey Dell again or have any communication with him!'

'Don't be so sure,' the girl replied. 'I'm of age: I could have married Harvey without your consent. I did the right thing because you're my father. Naturally, if Harvey asked for money — no matter how worthy the motive — you'd refuse. You even shy when *I* ask for a cheque. This decision of yours might change my whole life — if I let it.'

'You *will* let it!' Hammond said, eyes glinting.

16

'I don't think so, Father,' Claire got to her feet. Hammond knew by her change from 'dad' to 'father' that he had a fight on his hands.

'Claire . . . ' He gripped her small, dainty hands. 'I'm a man of the world. I've spent three times your years in dealing with smart alecks and get-rich-quicks of all descriptions. You're only young, and susceptible. In your position you are known to be wealthy, as my daughter. Undesirables are bound to be attracted and — '

'You've said enough, Father. I *know* Harvey, and you don't. And if I want to see him it will take more than you to stop me.'

She swept out of the room. Benson T. Hammond stood breathing hard, dark fury on his face as the door slammed shut.

★　★　★

Harvey Dell's bachelor flat was in Cadogan Place, off Sloane Street, but he made no attempt to go there on leaving

17

Hammond's residence. Instead he drove his car slowly, pondering, the windscreen wiper clearing the persistent misty drizzle from the glass. Once or twice, in the rear mirror, he caught sight of two car sidelights, which never seemed to come any nearer.

Instead of driving straight into the city he branched off and dodged up and down side roads until he came into Stanton Street in the Bayswater area. The two lights were still behind him at the same distance.

Stanton Street was composed of one row of solid Georgian-type houses eighteen in all, in blocks of six. The short street contained eighteen houses on one side and an empty, boarded up derelict site on the other. Two of the blocks of six houses each were obviously tenanted — the remaining block of six was not, except for the one at the far end. The five houses that remained had decay and neglect on their filthy exteriors; crosswise planks covered where windows should have been.

In the endmost house the windows

were intact and dim light showed pinkly from behind the curtains in the lower front room. Harvey stopped his car outside number nine, and the two sidelights which had apparently been following him all the way from Maida Vale grew bigger in the rear mirror and swung sideways as the car went on its way. He stared after it as the car went round the corner of the short street and vanished.

Harvey left his car and walked up the short pathway of number nine. A small portico was at the top of three steps. He mounted them and rang the old-fashioned bell. Just then a large car came sweeping back through Stanton Street and kept on going until it was lost to sight. Harvey frowned — then he rang the bell again persistently. Three long pulls.

Silence, but the dim light behind the front-room curtains indicated occupancy. The door opened very slightly, a rattling chain checking its swing.

'Okay, Les, it's Harvey,' Harvey said briefly.

The chain was freed and Harvey stepped into a dimly lighted hall. A low-powered lamp slung on a piece of flex and hanging beside the normal bulbless fitting cast down a yellow glimmer on to a man's fair head. He was broad-shouldered and in a tweed suit.

'Well?' he asked quietly, locking the front door behind them. 'What's the answer?'

'The answer is no,' Harvey replied. 'Not only to my request, but also my engagement to Claire. I was ordered out and told never to go back.'

Silence in the shadowy gloom. There was an intense smell of dust and, remotely, like something more imagined than noticed, an odour like ozone.

'We might have known it,' said the man under the lamp. 'That grasping old devil wouldn't help a drowning kitten even if he were in the same damned water-butt. Well, now we know. What are you going to do about it?'

'I'll have to think it out,' Harvey responded. 'I don't think Claire will stand for it, and if not the door may not be entirely closed after all. I'll ring up Cliff and tell him what's happened, and he isn't going to be any more pleased than I am.'

2

To Hammond's relief he found Claire present at dinner that evening as usual. That she had not left the house in pursuit of Harvey Dell was because she had recalled that Harvey had said he would write her. Reflection had decided her to wait for the mail to arrive. Harvey's own explanation should enable her to get matters into a clearer perspective.

Usually both Claire and her father engaged in spirited conversation — dinner being about the only time when they were together — but tonight Claire said not a word.

In the lounge afterwards it was no different. Claire spent the time absorbed in a novel and never spoke. She ignored him when at last her father rose and glanced at the clock.

'I hope that you realize how childish you are being, Claire?'

'I'm quite grown up,' she snapped.

'How much so you'll find out before long.'

Hammond's florid face darkened as he left the room.

Claire was down early next morning, anxiously awaiting the mail. The hours passed in worrying indecision. Then her uncertainties were set at rest as the postman brought the letter she was expecting, penned in Harvey's unmistakable hand. Evidently he had — as she'd hoped — posted it at the General Post Office, where there was a late night collection.

Taking the letter into the lounge, she tore the envelope quickly and pulled the notepaper out. Her eagerness faded slowly into wonder as she read the lines:

Flat 96,
70 Cadogan Place, S.W.1.
Monday night.
Dearest Claire,

Being local, this letter should reach you during tomorrow, when your father is at business. I would have phoned, only I don't trust telephones for what I have to say to you . . . Nor can I fully explain everything in this letter. It is very important that I should see you — but not at my usual flat.

I want you to meet me at 9 Stanton St., W.2. When you arrive I'll explain the exact reason for this queer subterfuge, but I don't want to give away too much in black and white. Since that which I have to explain to you is a secret I would be glad if you would come alone, without car and chauffeur: take a taxi. Remember, do not give the number you want in Stanton Street to anybody, not even to the taxi-driver. Get out at the street corner and walk along to number 9.

Finally, destroy this letter. No reason why your father should read it ... seven-thirty tonight, then, at 9 Stanton Street. Should you decide against coming, though you have absolutely nothing to fear, I'll get in touch with you again later. Believe me, I really have got something thrilling to tell you!

Always yours,
Harvey.

Claire frowned. A thought occurred to her and she hurried up to her bedroom. She closed the door, pushed aside the glass bowls and tray on the dressing table, and then went to her wardrobe. From the bottom of it she took out a steel cash box, unlocked it, and produced a bundle of Harvey's old letters.

Selecting three, she laid them out on the cleared dressing table beside Harvey's latest letter and compared the handwriting. It *was* Harvey's handwriting — on his own embossed notepaper. Queer, though, about this new address in Stanton Street. But since he was evidently entrusting her with some kind of secret, there was apparently nothing to fear.

She tore the note up into shreds and threw them in the wastebasket under the telephone table. Harvey had said seven-thirty. That meant she must be out of the house before six when her father came home, otherwise he would ask all manner of annoying questions.

Claire put the letters away in the cash box and returned it to the wardrobe, then she began dressing for the outdoors. Twenty minutes later she descended the staircase. Her hope of slipping out unseen was forestalled by Hilton as he crossed the hall from the lounge.

'If my father should inquire, Hilton, I'm going into town,' she improvised.

'Yes, miss. Shall I have the car — '

'I'm not using the car. Seems to me it's time I had a little exercise.'

'Yes, miss.' Hilton looked at her in vaguely wondering respect. Claire left the house, went hurriedly down the drive in the clinging reek of the already darkening November afternoon.

She was considering the unfamiliar prospect of taking a bus into town when a passing taxi solved the problem for her. She climbed into it and in fifteen minutes was in the city. There was ample time to window-gaze and then go somewhere for tea.

She followed out her own plan exactly, arranging matters so that another taxi brought her to the end of the dilapidated Stanton Street at seven twenty-five.

'This is it, miss,' the taxi-driver said,

holding the door of the vehicle open for her.

Claire alighted slowly and looked about her. 'Pretty dreary-looking spot, isn't it?'

'Mostly condemned property around 'ere, miss. Most of these 'ouses is empty. What 'ouse do you want? I could drive you to it.'

'No, never mind — thanks all the same.' Claire handed over the fare and a liberal tip. The taxi driver returned to his cab and drove off. Moments later the sound of another car caught her attention.

She had noticed it when she had alighted to the pavement. It had been parked at the other end of the street. Now it suddenly began moving, turned completely round, and came speeding towards her. Despite the indifferent street lighting and the fact that it was on the opposite side of the road, Claire recognized it immediately.

'Harvey!' she cried, raising her hand and waving. '*Harvey!*'

If it was Harvey at the wheel he took no notice. Through the steamy car windows she could only vaguely descry the form of a man, then the car had swung round the corner — but as it went Claire had a clear vision of the rear number plate.

Even if it had not been Harvey, it certainly had been his car. She knew his registration number by heart. Then the house outside which the car had been parked was probably the one she was seeking . . . With a deepening sense of wonder, even of alarm, she crossed the wet, gleaming road and began to walk along the pavement, gazing about her upon the decrepit property.

Once she had passed the two blocks that were obviously tenanted it was as though she had walked into a dead world. The rottenness had become a festering thing. The great Georgian houses, but faintly lighted by the street lamps, loomed around her, mysterious, abandoned, with their huge wooden Xs where glass had been in the windows. Not another person anywhere.

Presently she stopped to consider the number on a gatepost. The endmost house, with dim light behind drawn curtains. Number nine. Quickly she went up the short length of path, up the steps to the portico. The rusty iron knob of the old-fashioned bell was visible in a counter-sunk hole in the masonry. She pulled at it fiercely and listened. There did not seem to be any answering ring from the depths of the archaic place.

The front room seemed to be occupied, though with the curtains tightly drawn there was no chance of seeing within. As nobody answered her ringing she stepped back and gazed up at the house's upper reaches, a fine drizzle descending into her face. There were no lights up there, and if there were curtains it was too dark to see them.

Puzzled, she stepped over a line of low half-moon-shaped wires, separating the flagged pathway from a weedy patch of garden. Reaching the big front windows she suddenly felt her shoes give back a metallic ring. She glanced down and the dim street lamp gave back the reflection of wet iron grating bars. Evidently the house had a basement. Not that she could see anything below. It was blacker than Erebus . . .

A sudden voice halted her. 'What do you want?'

With a little gasp she turned. There was a man standing on the topmost step under the portico — a shadowy figure and extremely tall.

'I — I was just looking round,' Claire explained.

The man did not answer. He backed slightly into the hall of the house so that a single dim glimmering lamp cast upon him. All Claire could see was polished dark hair, then white spots in a dark triangle, which indicated the man's forehead, high cheekbones, and chin. He appeared to have a frockcoat and there was a vague suggestion of striped trousers.

Claire smiled nervously. 'I was just curious. I can't think why Harvey — Mr. Dell, my fiancé — should ask me to come here.'

'I never heard the name,' the manservant — for such he seemed to be — responded. 'There must be some mistake.'

'This is number nine Stanton Street, isn't it?'

'It is,' the manservant acknowledged. 'But I never heard of a Mr. Dell. Unless the master is using some other kind of name. Have you a letter from him, or some form of introduction?'

'Look here,' Claire demanded, 'Mr. Dell sent me a letter, asking me to come here for seven-thirty, and he told me to destroy the letter, which I did. How can I be expected to have it with me?'

Silence.

'Who is your master, anyway?' Claire snapped.

'I am not at liberty to answer that question, miss, any more than I am at liberty to admit you — '

'But I'm Claire Hammond,' Claire insisted. 'I refuse to be put off. If Mr. Dell isn't in I'll come in and wait. I think I saw him leave in his car only a few minutes ago, only he didn't see me.'

'I'm sorry, miss, but there is nothing I can do.'

The door slammed suddenly.

Claire turned to the bell and pulled at

it repeatedly until at last she was forced to admit herself beaten. Baffled, she stared at the heavily curtained windows and then went slowly down the pathway to the pavement and glanced along the street.

'If this is his idea of a joke I'll give him something to go on with!' she breathed venomously. 'I'll show *him*!'

She began walking actively. At the main road she ought to be able to get a taxi. Her only thought was to be whirled to Harvey's flat and there demand an explanation — and she hoped for Harvey's own sake that it would prove to be a good one.

★　★　★

At six o'clock Benson T. Hammond entered the hall of his home and the impassive Hilton helped him to remove his hat and coat.

'Unpleasant weather, Hilton,' Hammond commented, casting a brief look about him in order to be assured that the servants had done their work properly.

'Indeed it is, sir. Most unpleasant.'

'Any mail during the day?'

'Not for you, sir. There was a letter for Miss Claire.'

'Oh? Mmmm . . . Any callers?'

'None, sir.'

'Very well. Dinner at eight as usual. I'll be in my study if I'm needed. You might ask my daughter to come and have a word with me, will you?'

'I'm afraid Miss Claire is not at home, sir. She said she was going into town, should you inquire.' Hilton hesitated. 'She did not take the car. She made some remark about needing exercise.'

'All right, Hilton, that will be all.'

Into town? Without the car? Hammond frowned.

He hurried up the staircase to Claire's room. Flinging open the door, he switched on the light and stood gazing about him upon the essentially feminine appointments. He went over to the wardrobe and pulled open the doors. It seemed to him that few or none of garments had been removed. The wardrobe was filled with them.

Hammond searched round until he

came to Claire's ox-hide suitcases inside the massive ottoman at the foot of the bed.

The thought that she might have decided to walk out — and stay out — began to recede. If she came back he could deal with the situation — unless she came back married to Harvey Dell by special license.

'She'd do it too!' Hammond clenched his fists. 'Something made her decide on this suddenly. Letter, eh? Was it from Harvey? Damn — be in her handbag now . . .'

He stood thinking; then the curious disarrangement of the dressing-table top caught his attention. The cut glass brush-tray and powder bowls had been pushed to the rear. The silver-backed brush and comb, which he had given her for her twenty-first birthday, were perched insecurely. The whole effect was that the contents of the dressing table top had been pushed on one side to make room — for something. As indeed they had when Claire had compared her letter with Harvey's earlier notes. In her haste she had forgotten to rearrange the disorder.

Hammond realized it could only have happened since morning or the maid would have put things straight. His eyes travelled leftwards to the telephone on its little table, the scratchpad beside it — then dropped to the wastebasket. The torn shreds of paper caught his eye, and he dived down a hand.

He laid the paper pieces on top of the dressing table and began looking at each one in turn. Certain fragments arrested his interest. 'Monday night', and underneath it, 'letter should . . . is at business . . . ephones'. Another bit said, ' . . . est Claire, Being local . . . '

Hammond whirled up a chair and began a careful fitting-together of the jigsaw. It took him an hour. When he had the letter complete he read it through and then went down to his study for gummed labels. Coming back to the bedroom with them, he transferred the pieces to the adhesive surfaces of the labels and built the letter up into completeness.

'Number nine Stanton Street?' he

repeated in wonder. 'I can't imagine what that young upstart's doing there. He's up to something, and Claire's been crazy enough to run after him . . . Seven-thirty.'

He glanced at his watch: seven-twenty. He put the jigsaw letter in his wallet, then hurried downstairs. He rang for Hilton.

'Tell Simmons to get the car out immediately,' he ordered. 'I've an urgent appointment. I may be late back for dinner.'

'Yes, sir . . . ' Hilton moved a little quicker than usual.

'Just a chance that I can catch her,' Hammond breathed. 'I'll stop that fortune-hunting young swine if it's the last thing I do!'

* * *

At the far end of the crescent-shaped road in which the Hammond residence stood, was a sleek black car dewed with the inclemency of the night. It was so placed that the two men inside it could distinctly see the tall, imposing gateway of the Hammond house without themselves attracting attention. They were two plainclothes men, detailed to keep guard over a frightened shipping magnate.

'I'm sick of this,' the man at the wheel muttered, and scraped a match to light the cigarettes of himself and his companion.

'Oh, I don't know.' The other was more philosophic. 'At least we're quite dry in the car.'

'Roll on tomorrow night,' said the man at the wheel. 'We're due to be relieved. This is pointless — but the old man must be obeyed.'

The non-philosophic plainclothes man promptly consigned the old man — alias Chief Inspector Garth of the Yard — to the devil, and drew hard at his cigarette. Detective-inspector Billings preferred action and something that taxed his brains. With his companion, Detective-sergeant Cassell, it was different. He could be interested in apparently nothing whatever and then write a treatise about it. But even he would admit that there *were* better ways of spending a November night.

'Not by any means as interesting as last night,' Cassell commented presently. 'At least we had that bloke to follow as far as Stanton Street. Not that it meant anything, but it was a change . . . Y'know, I can't fathom whether the old man approved of us doing that or not.'

'Never can tell with Garth,' Billings sighed. 'He raised hell because it's our job to watch Hammond, not to follow the characters who visit him. All right — whoever comes or goes we'll stick exclusively to Hammond in future . . . S'pose we did make a mess of it last night, really. We only followed Harvey Dell after all, and he's a friend of the family. Thank God nothing happened to Hammond at his home here whilst we were following Dell or we'd have been kicked off the force — '

'Hey, take a look!' Cassell interrupted, sitting up.

The shining bonnet of Hammond's limousine was emerging from the gateway of the residence. The whole length of the car gradually glided into view and then went off down the road, its red rear light gleaming brilliantly.

'That Hammond, do you think?' Cassell asked sharply.

'It's his car, anyway,' Billings responded. 'Better follow it. Hurry up, before he gets lost in the traffic.'

By the time Cassell had driven to the end of the street the limousine had joined the city traffic on the major road. The moment there was a clear space Cassell shot across the road, accelerated, and after several overtakes finally came within a respectable distance of the fast-speeding limousine and kept it in sight.

'Know something?' Cassell murmured, as he swung the car swiftly round corner after corner chasing the limousine through quieter side streets. 'I believe we're heading for the same spot as last night when we followed Harvey Dell. We're getting to that district now.'

Ten minutes later the limousine turned into the short, dreary length of Stanton Street, moved slowly along it, and finally halted.

'Same house as Dell visited last night,' Billings commented, as Cassell braked on the street corner. 'Something queer about that dump but I'll be damned if I know what — Hallo, there he goes!'

The broad figure of the shipper was visible for a moment alighting from the limousine. He stood contemplating the street and the house, and then he vanished through the gateway.

'Exactly seven-forty,' Billings said, glancing at the dashboard clock. 'That'll have to go in the report.'

'Do we sit here and wait 'til he comes out?' Cassell questioned

'What else? His car's waiting, and our job is to keep him under observation. Nothing more we can do.'

Nobody came or went in the badly lighted street. Now and again a car or taxi passed through, but that was all. The demolished-site loomed black and deserted.

Eight-thirty came, then eight-forty-five. Evidently the chauffeur had become worried too for he was visible now walking slowly up and down beside the limousine and glancing at the house.

'I don't like this,' Billings said abruptly.

'Drive up to the house.' The moment the car stopped Billings jumped out and walked across to the pacing chauffeur.

'We're from Scotland Yard,' Billings said, displaying his warrant card. 'Waiting for Mr. Hammond?'

The man nodded nervously. 'I don't understand it, officer. Mr. Hammond said he'd only be a few minutes. It's a full hour since he went in. Maybe I should have done something — knocked perhaps — when the front room had a light in it.'

'Light?' Billings repeated sharply.

The chauffeur nodded to the dark lower windows. 'When we first got here there was light behind the curtains. They showed up pinkish. After the master had been in the house for about ten or fifteen minutes the light suddenly went out. I assumed it was perhaps because they had gone into another room or something.'

'I suppose somebody let Mr. Hammond in?' Billings asked.

'Yes. I saw him — just,' the chauffeur amended. 'It was dark from where I was seated in the car here. I could see the dim outline of a very tall man against a single yellow light in the hall. Then Mr. Hammond went in and the door closed . . . ' The chauffeur frowned. 'What are the police doing here?'

'Our job is to keep an eye on Mr. Hammond and be sure he's safe,' Billings explained, 'and I don't like the look of this. Come on . . . '

He hurried up the front pathway, stopped under the portico and pressed on the ancient bell knob. There was no sound of pealing from anywhere within. Impatiently Billings raised his foot and kicked hard and reverberatingly on the weather-stained door. The noise went echoing into a seeming emptiness.

Billings made up his mind. 'We'll break the door in. In this case I think it's justified. Let's go!'

He signalled and all three flung their united strength against the warped and leprous wood. It took several lunges before they managed to tear the lock hasp free of its screws. Then they pulled up sharp in pitch darkness that reeked of dust and obscurely, of something resembling ozone.

'Anybody home?' Billings called, dragging out his torch and switching it on.

He halted. The torch beam was shining down a length of totally empty hall. There was not a stick of furniture anywhere. The walls were dirty and defaced where damp had crept in. At the limit of the hall was a staircase, uncarpeted, reaching up into a dark gulf . . .

Even more staggering was the fact that there was a thick even layer of dust on the floor of the hall. Nowhere was it broken by the marks of where any piece of furniture might have stood, nor was there a trace of a single footprint!

3

Simmons, the chauffeur, caught hold of Billings's arm. 'This is beyond — *reason*!' he declared, astounded. 'Whether you believe me or not, I tell you I saw Mr. Hammond enter this house when somebody asked him inside.'

'We saw it too,' Billings said tautly. 'Don't get excited.'

'What's *happened* here?' Simmons asked. 'It doesn't look as though anybody has been in this place for years! The dust's nearly half an inch thick.'

Billings pushed the front door to and raised his torch beam. It settled on an archaic type of single rod electrolier with a rusty bulb socket. Upon the electrolier and in the socket were filmy cobwebs.

'You said,' Billings said slowly, 'that you saw a light in the hall when Mr. Hammond was admitted?'

'Yes, I know I did. Hanging just about where that socket is. Dull yellow it was

— *very* dull. But it couldn't have been that! It's not been used since the Flood from the look of it.'

'What's happened to Hammond?' Cassell demanded. 'That's *our* worry!'

'Right,' Billings agreed. 'Let's see what we can find — Keep well to the side and don't disturb the dust any more than you can help. We'll try the front room.'

In single file close beside the skirting board, they entered the front room and also found it completely empty with a thick, undisturbed film of dust coating the floor and the unused and rusting grate. The dust was even in the air, twitching the nostrils.

In the ceiling Billings's torch beam revealed a twin electrolier, but similar to the one in the hall it was rusty and festooned with spiders' webs. What was more, both lamp sockets were missing. No bulbs could ever have been there.

'Not even any curtains!' the chauffeur exclaimed, as the beam moved on to the grimy windows.

They walked forward in the dust-hazed air, struggling not to sneeze. The window glass was dirty, preventing them seeing outside. The upwardly pointing torch beam revealed dirty woodwork round the windows with rusted nails, which had evidently been there for years. Of curtains or running rails there was no trace.

Everywhere they went the house was empty and thickly coated in dust upstairs and downstairs. The water was turned off at the mains and in a cupboard under the staircase both the gas and electricity meters had been sealed off by the suppliers.

'But there was a light in the front room, and in the hall!' Simmons insisted. 'I saw them!'

They next explored in the kitchen. The window, in common with all the windows in the house, was jammed tight with blistered paint. The back door had three bolts closed across it, all of them rusted into position.

'Nobody,' Billings announced solemnly, 'could have left this house except by the front door. And nobody did!'

'And according to this dust nobody has ever been *in* here, anyway!' Cassell pointed out perplexedly.

'What's that door there?' the chauffeur asked, pointing — and Billings swung the beam round upon a faded door in a corner, which so far they had all overlooked. He went across to it. It opened easily and beyond it were stone steps leading into darkness.

'Basement,' he said. 'Our last hope. Let's take a look.'

There were twelve stone steps in all, dust-covered. In the basement was a concrete floor with its inevitable layer of undisturbed dust. There was a fire-grate built into the wall. Upon the wall facing the fireplace was a big square of boarding.

'Better take a look at that,' Billings said, and they found it was composed of thick planking nailed and plugged into the wall. The nail heads were rusty but apparently of not very great age.

'Can't do anything with boarding without a jemmy or a chisel,' Cassell said. 'Certainly nobody went out this way. What about the fireplace?'

He crossed to it and Billings joined him, flashing the torch beam. The flue was too narrow to admit of a human being, and anyway it was choked with soot.

Billings motioned as his ever-probing beam fell on an uneven floor near the most distant wall. As they advanced they saw that it was caused by dust being piled on a circular cast-iron grating, sunk into the concrete floor. The grating was perhaps four feet in diameter and appeared to be hinged.

'Drain for this cellar?' Simmons hazarded.

'Seems a bit queer to have a drain this size to carry off water.' Billings said slowly. 'Large enough for a manhole . . . Give me a hand. See if we can raise it.'

They all hooked their fingers under the iron network and pulled fiercely, but the cover refused to budge.

'No use,' Billings sighed at last, desisting. He held up his hand. 'Hear something?'

Both men heard it too — the sound of swirling, bubbling water echoing up the wide shaft, at the top of which was this immovable, hinged iron grid.

'If anybody escaped down that, how did they do it without disturbing the dust on it?' the chauffeur demanded. 'And where in blazes is my boss?' he went on in alarm. 'Where *is* he?'

'You're as wise as we are,' Billings answered grimly. 'Cassell, you stay on guard and I'll get in touch with the Yard. The old man's going to love being dragged out of his home to investigate this lot . . . '

★　★　★

Andrew Morton, commercial traveler, was perfectly satisfied with life. The exclusive sale to a Brighton hotel of a new line in rubberoid floor covering meant considerable commission and therefore money on the side for the Christmas season.

Morton was humming to himself behind the wheel of his car as he sped along the coast road from Brighton through Portslade and Southwick. The time was seven-forty by the dashboard clock and he was reasonably sure that if he stepped on it he would be home in Worthing by eight.

It was as he left Shoreham behind that the brilliant headlights of his car picked out something unusual in the middle of the road perhaps five hundred yards distant. It looked like an extra large dog, which had perhaps been run over, or a sack dropped from a lorry. He slowed down and peered intently through the sickle cleaned in the glass by the wiper — Then with a gasp he jerked the car to a halt.

It was not a dog or a sack. It was a man, lying flat on his face.

Morton tumbled out into the drizzle, the road ahead lighted by his headlamps. To the left of him the sea was roaring. To the right were the mist and drizzle-shrouded downs with a dim vision of a solitary hut perching against a murky skyline. There was no sign of any other car on the road.

Morton gripped the man by the shoulders and raised him up. He was fairly heavily built, probably not very tall when standing, and expensively dressed in a blue melton overcoat and black Homburg.

'Is anything wrong ... ?' Morton stopped, his eyes starting.

Two things were appalling him. First there was the fact that the man appeared to be dead; and secondly that his shoulders and arms were somehow *soggy*. Morton could think of no other term. The flesh seemed to slide and slip as though no bones were holding it in place. Instead of gripping a body it was more like gripping a partially deflated inner tube. The man's arm, when Morton seized it, bent into an incredible U-shape, like that of a rag doll. Morton could be forgiven for letting go hastily, nearly jerked out of sanity in his amazement.

He took a few steps backwards and then by sheer self-compulsion forced himself to return. He had to do something, even if the man had been run over already which accounted for the broken bones.

Finally Morton seized the man by the shoulders of his coat and dragged him to the side of the road where he flopped and sprawled incredibly as if filled with water.

Andrew Morton glanced about him worriedly. Now he had found the body he wanted to stay beside it: it might get his name in the papers and become a useful topic to start conversation whilst he made a sale . . . Couldn't accuse *him* of running the man down, anyway. If he *had* been run down. He could tell the driver of the next bus going to Worthing to inform the police.

Morton looked at his watch. It was ten minutes to eight. That meant at least ten minutes before a bus came past.

'Can't wait that long,' he muttered. 'This is urgent.'

He was in a quandary. To look for the nearest telephone would mean leaving the body. He debated the idea of dragging the body into his car and driving it to the nearest police station, then he recalled hazily that the police like to see a body untouched, if possible, on the actual spot where it is lying. They could hardly blame him for dragging it from the middle of the road, but to take it to a police station might be asking for it.

The problem resolved itself as a girl on a pedal cycle, dressed in a transparent plastic mackintosh and hood, came wobbling into the area of the headlights.

'Hey, miss! Just a moment!'

The girl zigzagged to a stop and put one foot down on the road. She looked in surprise at Morton standing beside the sprawled body at the side of the road. Then surprise changed to fright and she endeavored to remount her machine, stumbled, and slid off. Morton came over to her as she struggled to straighten the bicycle.

'Don't get scared,' he snapped. 'I want help — and quickly. Are you going in the Worthing direction?'

'Uh-huh . . . ' She gazed at him with wide eyes.

'Stop at the first police station and tell them to send somebody here at once — with a doctor. I've found a dead man lying in the road. Tell 'em that.'

'D-dead? Oh, Lor'!' The girl scrambled back on to the saddle. 'Yes, all right, I'll tell 'em. I — I can't be very quick, though. This confounded wind's against me.'

'Do the best you can.'

Morton watched the rear lamp of the cycle until it vanished, then he went back to his car and drove it forward until it was beside the body. He switched off the headlights and remained in the driving seat, waiting.

The dashboard clock crept on to eight-ten. Two buses passed him, going in opposite directions. Cars seemed to be non-existent tonight, just when he could have done with one to carry a message quickly. Then through the dewed windscreen he caught sight of a car approaching rapidly from the Worthing direction, a purple-lettered sign on its roof. The letters took on outline and said POLICE.

Morton stepped out into the road, drawing his head into his collar as the drizzle soaked him. The car drew in swiftly to one side and halted.

An inspector in uniform accompanied by a sergeant came hurrying over to him.

He motioned. Words were unnecessary. In silence he stood watching the two kneeling figures as they examined the corpse.

'The police doctor will be here soon with an ambulance,' the inspector said presently, rising. 'The girl you sent said you found this body lying in the road . . . Whereabouts, sir?'

Morton indicated the spot. 'I hope I didn't do wrong, Inspector, pulling him — I mean it — clear of the traffic?'

'No; it was the only thing you could do.' The inspector frowned. 'Something queer here, though. Seems as though he's been run over several times. Maybe you noticed? His flesh is — '

'Yes.' Morton's voice had an odd intonation. 'I noticed.'

The inspector examined a wallet in the combined lights of the two cars. From it he presently removed a visiting card.

'Benson T. Hammond,' he said slowly. 'Kensal Height, Maida Vale London . . . So that's who he is — or was. Well, sir I'd better take a few particulars whilst I'm waiting.'

★ ★ ★

Chief Inspector Garth was standing at the top of the stone steps that led into the basement of number nine Stanton Street. Around him stood Sergeant Whittaker, Cassell, and Billings each holding torches . . . Only the chauffeur was absent. After taking a statement from him Garth had sent him packing, with instructions to keep his mouth shut.

Garth frowned and glanced about the dimly lighted kitchen. 'I'll have a look in the basement here, though I don't expect to find anything more than you chaps have. You go first, Cassell, with that torch.'

Cassell led the descent. Garth followed to the base of the steps and then stood looking at the boarding on the wall opposite the fireplace.

'That's why I asked for a jemmy or a tire-lever, sir,' Cassell explained. 'Not that it will solve the problem of what has happened to Hammond, or explain where the man who let him in here has gone, but — '

'Got that tire-lever, Whitty?' Garth glanced back over his shoulder at the detective-sergeant.

'Right here, sir.' Whittaker pulled it from his overcoat.

'Okay — go to work on that boarding and let's see what we can get.'

Garth took the torches and Cassell and Billings went over to help Whittaker. The chief inspector stood watching in the torchlight as the three men worked on the boarding. Between them they finally wrenched the boards away with a deafening squeak of nails. A grimy window, the glass intact, became visible. Cassell retrieved his torch and flashed it through the glass into a kind of square well, then the beam moved upwards to a grating beyond which was a hazy view of the sky.

'Nothing sir, except a window,' Cassell announced. 'Seems to be a grating in the front garden belonging to it. The window is all in one piece. Nobody came or went this way. And the chimney's blocked up, and narrow, as I told you.'

Garth looked at the wood that had

been torn down and then at the nails with which it had been fastened. 'At least this part of the riddle isn't as rusty as the rest,' he commented. 'I'd say these boards were put up fairly recently.'

'But why?' Whittaker asked. 'Why block a window which is already protected by a grating and the fact that the window is not of the opening variety?'

Garth grinned. 'To prevent anybody seeing *in* here, of course!'

'Yes . . . ' Whittaker rubbed the back of his thick neck.

'Let's have a look at this manhole cover . . . ' Garth strode over to it and the others followed with the torches. Garth stooped, hooked his fingers in the grid's metalwork, and pulled futilely.

'Either extremely heavy, or jammed,' Cassell said.

'It's not that heavy — it's only three inches thick and hinged,' Garth growled.

He squatted, musing; then he took the stub of his cheroot from his teeth and dropped it cleanly through the grid. The red point sailed down into remoteness and expired. The noise of gurgling water came floating up.

'Roughly thirty feet depth,' Garth said, glancing. He lowered his face towards the grating and sniffed hard. Then he looked puzzled. 'This can't be a sewer — no odour.'

'Looks like this manhole cover hasn't been touched for ages,' Cassell said. 'Look at the dust on it! And that dust was even and undisturbed when Billings and I first looked at it.'

'Uh-huh,' Garth agreed. 'And I also notice that on the underside of this grid there is a bolt driven home. I can just see the hooked end of it sticking out . . . No wonder we can't raise it.'

'I don't see how anybody could bolt this manhole cover when there is a thirty-foot shaft below, four feet in width,' Whittaker said. 'Seems to suggest that whoever did it must have hung in mid air.'

'Nobody *could* come up from below,' Cassell remarked. 'And it looks from the undisturbed dust as though nobody did anything from above, either.'

Garth took the torch from Cassell and

flashed the ray along the basement ceiling. It was composed of smooth, dirty plaster with no trace of a beam, hook, or any other device.

Silence, the smell of dust, the distant gurgle of water, and the steady breathing of four baffled men.

Garth glared around him. 'It's uncanny! Hammond was seen to be admitted to this house. Nobody came out the front way — the only possible way — and we find the house smothered in dust half an inch thick, the meters sealed off, and a manhole cover bolted underneath at the top of a thirty-foot shaft.' He motioned to the staircase.

'Nothing more we can do here. Let's get up above and see what we can think of. First call will be at Hammond's place to see why he came here — if anybody knows.'

Bad-tempered, Garth led the way up the stone steps, through the dusty hall, and into the open. He glanced at Cassell and Billings. 'You two boys had better stay here until you're relieved. If anybody should come, get all particulars and advise me. In case I'm needed I'm going to Hammond's place, then on to the Yard.'

He turned and strode down the path to the waiting police car. He paused beside it and watched with Whittaker as another fast patrol car came speeding into view and stopped. A uniformed inspector climbed out.

'Glad to have caught you, sir.' The inspector saluted. 'I picked up a short-wave from the Yard asking that you be contacted immediately. It's urgent — something to do with Hammond. You're to ring Worthing seven-nine right away.'

'Hammond?' Garth alerted. 'Get this crate back to the Yard, Whitty, fast as you can. Better see what all his is about before we go to Hammond's place.'

The car sped through the glazed, drizzly streets towards Scotland Yard, Whittaker driving. Reaching his office, Garth went to the telephone and whipped it up.

'Get me Worthing seven-nine right away,' he instructed, and half-perched himself on the big desk. Whittaker, standing near him, saw bafflement in the pale blue eyes. 'Yes? Yes? Who's that? This is Chief Inspector Garth.'

'Inspector Grimshaw of the Worthing police here, sir. We've been advised about a body on the Worthing-Shoreham road — apparently run over. Particulars in the man's wallet say he's Benson T. Hammond of Kensal Height, Maida Vale. I rang up the Divisional Inspector — F Division — and asked him to have Hammond's relatives advised. Instead he referred me to you and says there is some police protection you are giving. He seemed to know of it because you'd asked him to try and trace some mysterious threatening letters Hammond had been receiving . . . What are my instructions, sir?'

'Wait a minute!' Garth breathed. 'Let me get this straight — Did you say *Benson T. Hammond*?'

'Yes, sir. I got his name from the cards in his wallet and — '

'Forget that. What does he look like?'

'About five feet seven, squarely built, florid-faced, aged between fifty-five and sixty. Blue melton overcoat and a

Homburg hat. He was found on the main coast road between Shoreham and Worthing. A commercial by the name of Andrew Morton found him and sent a girl cyclist to advise us.'

'What time was the body found?'

'Morton says he discovered it at ten to eight. He remembers that he looked at his dashboard clock . . . I think you'd better come over here, sir. There's a lot of interesting things in Hammond's wallet, and there is also something odd about him. Apart from a fractured skull, which our police surgeon says has been caused by our old friend the blunt instrument, Hammond's bones seem as though they've turned to jelly.'

'Jelly?' Garth repeated blankly; then he got a hold of himself. 'All right, I'll be there as quickly as I can.'

He put down the phone and slid from the edge of the desk. 'Whitty, I must be dreaming. This business is utterly *impossible!*'

Not having heard the Worthing end of the conversation, Whittaker merely looked vague.

'Listen to this, my lad. At twenty to eight Hammond went into that problem house in Stanton Street — and two perfectly reliable plainclothes men and a chauffeur saw him do it. He never came out. At ten to eight — ten minutes later — his body was found on the main coast road between Shoreham and Worthing, his skull cracked and his bones somehow jellied.'

'But . . . ' Whittaker stared. 'It can't be Hammond! Why, it's nearly sixty miles from here to Worthing . . . Sixty miles in ten minutes! And nobody ever came out of that house in Stanton Street.'

'Let's get down to Worthing before we think of ordering strait-jackets,' Garth said.

4

At nine o'clock this same evening Harvey Dell was seated in a drive-in café on the main road through Redhill. Often, on journeys to see his friend Jimmy Mitchell in Lancing — midway between Worthing and Shoreham — he had broken the trip here. Catering chiefly for lorry drivers and long-distance bus services, it was open day and night.

'Going far tonight, Mr. Dell?'

It was Montrose, the proprietor, who had asked the question. He was leaning his bulk on the glass-topped counter, surrounded by tall dishes loaded up with pies, cakes, and meat-paste sandwiches. Behind him hissed the coffee, tea, and hot-water urns.

'Far enough,' Harvey Dell answered, pondering. 'But in fact I don't think there's much point in my carrying on. It's a filthy night . . . Best thing I can do is skip back to London before the weather gets any worse. I was going to drive over to Lancing, but there's a mist coming up. Not worth the risk and the time.'

He got to his feet, buttoning up his overcoat. Crossing to the counter, he paid for his coffee and biscuits.

'See you again,' he said.

'Good night, Mr. Dell.'

Thoughtfully, Harvey wandered out of the long, shack-like building to his car. 'I suppose Jimmy'll judge for himself that things haven't turned out right,' he muttered. 'In fact he'll have to.'

He returned to London, driving his car into the enormous garage provided for the block of flats in which he lived. It was quarter to ten when he entered the main hall of the apartment building and took the self-service lift to the third floor. As he stepped from the lift he saw a figure seated at the far end of the well-carpeted corridor.

Claire Hammond was resting on one of the corridor chairs outside the door of his flat. She stood up as he appeared, dark anger on her face, her fur coat flowing loose in the warmth of the building.

'About time,' she said laconically. 'I've been stuck waiting here since just after eight o'clock! I'm waiting for your explanation!'

Harvey hesitated and glanced towards the door of his flat as there came the sound of a telephone.

'That's been ringing at intervals throughout the evening,' Claire told him. 'Look here Harvey, why did you send me that fool note and set me off on a wild-goose chase?'

'Tell you in a moment,' Harvey answered, unlocking the flat door. 'Let's see who's calling first . . .'

Inside he switched on the light and hurried over to the instrument. 'Yes? Harvey Dell here . . .' Claire wandered into the well-furnished lounge and closed the main door. She waited impatiently.

'He did, eh?' Harvey asked, as a voice muttered inaudibly over the wire. 'Eh . . . ? Yes, I see what you mean . . .'

Harvey's expression changed from frowning interest to one of wonder — and then into blank amazement. He even looked horrified. Claire studied the metamorphosis in silent but puzzled interest.

'You *did*?' Harvey gasped finally. 'But dammit all, man — Yes, yes, I know, but . . . Good heavens!' Harvey finished blankly. 'I — I'll have to think it out. Yes, leave it at that . . . ' He put the telephone down and stood lost in thought.

'If you've quite finished,' Claire reminded him, 'I'm still waiting. You said you'd explain about that note you sent me.'

'Note? What are you talking about, Claire?'

'Talking about? But when we came in here you said you'd explain after answering that phone call.'

Harvey motioned Claire to sit down on the chesterfield and then went across to the cocktail cabinet. She took the drink he gave her and watched him whilst he downed a neat brandy.

'That's better,' he said, putting the glass back on the cabinet.

'Glad something is,' Claire commented sourly. 'Now, what was the idea of asking me to go to nine Stanton Street when you knew you would never be there to meet me?'

'I asked you to?' Harvey questioned.

'You know perfectly well that you did! On your own notepaper — and in your own handwriting, too. I checked it against some of your earlier letters. You asked me to call at nine Stanton Street this evening, about seven-thirty, because you had something very important to tell me. I went — and somebody who looked like a manservant told me that he had never heard of you.'

Harvey frowned. 'You're sure you didn't dream all this, dearest?'

'Dream it?' Claire's voice went up an octave. 'Of course I didn't! I — '

'I'd like to see that note,' Harvey said, thinking.

'But I destroyed it. You told me to in case Dad happened to see it. So I tore it in bits and threw it in the wastepaper basket in my bedroom. You needn't worry: nobody'll ever find it.'

'But I *am* worrying! I want to see it, if only to try and find out what on earth you're talking about.'

Claire got to her feet, slamming down the brandy-and-soda fiercely; half the liquid slopped over on to her hand.

'I don't know whether this is a practical joke or an elaborate brush-off,' she said coldly, 'but either way it's a pretty rotten way to treat me, Harvey. It's no use you denying it about nine Stanton Street, either, because as I was getting from the taxi tonight, I saw your car leave that very house.'

'My car?' Harvey exclaimed.

'Yours! It had your registration number. Whether it was you driving it or not I don't know because the windows of the car were steamy, the lighting was bad, and — Well, you took no notice when I shouted . . . Harvey, what does it all mean?'

'You must have been dreaming — or else you have been thoroughly hoaxed. I never sent that letter.'

'Then who did? And how did that person get hold of your own embossed notepaper and imitate your handwriting?'

'I dunno. Lots of people come here: one of them could have pinched a piece of notepaper any time. As for handwriting, that isn't so hard to imitate.'

'Yours is: it's a scrawl! It would take a master forger to imitate it.' The cold, offended gleam was still in the girl's eyes. 'And your car?' she questioned.

'It wasn't mine. Same make maybe; that's more than possible, but as for the registration number — '

'It was *your number*! I've got eyes, Harvey, and I didn't imagine anything . . . What sort of a game do you call this? Evidently Dad was right in his judgment of you. You're nothing but a — a liar!'

'Look here, Claire — '

'And don't ever try to speak to me again!' she snapped, swinging to the door, and slamming it behind her.

Harvey stood, anger flooding his face, then he strode over to the footstool near the fireplace and took a running kick at it. He watched it bounce into a corner. For the moment it satisfied his emotions, then he returned to the telephone and raised it.

'Lancing, seven-six,' he told the operator, and waited moodily until a voice

71

answered. 'Mr. Mitchell there?' he asked, and listened. 'He isn't? Well, would you mind asking him to ring Mr. Dell the moment he comes in? Tell him it's extremely urgent. It doesn't matter what time it is . . . Yes, that's it. Thanks.'

★　★　★

Under the cold, pitiless glare of the lights in the Worthing mortuary Chief Inspector Garth stood looking at the sheet that covered the body of Benson T. Hammond. It had just been drawn back into place by the hand of Inspector Grimshaw. Detective-sergeant Whittaker stood biting his lower lip.

'Yes,' Garth said, 'that's Hammond all right. Just the same he'll have to be identified by a member of his family. Only be his daughter for it. I suppose you've advised her what's happened?'

'I tried to, but the butler said that Miss Hammond was out somewhere and that he'd tell her the moment she returned. I have of course informed the Worthing coroner.'

Garth scowled. 'So the butler is going to tell Miss Hammond, is he? That'll be a nice treat for her when she comes in. I'd better ring her up and see if I can smooth the path for her.'

'Okay,' Grimshaw agreed. 'Let's be getting back to my office.'

In a trio they went out to Grimshaw's official car and a sergeant drove them to police headquarters in the centre of the town. Entering his private office, Grimshaw put a call through to the Hammond home.

Pause. 'I'd like to speak to Miss Hammond, please,' Grimshaw said suddenly. 'Yes, it's the Worthing police again . . . Yes, I'll wait.' Pause. 'Miss Hammond?' Grimshaw asked, and handed the phone to Garth.

'Hallo, Miss Hammond,' Garth said, his voice sombre. 'This is Inspector Garth of the C.I.D. speaking . . . '

'Garth, did you say?' Claire Hammond's voice sounded agitated. 'You mean Chief Inspector Garth? Daddy's friend?'

'I *was* his friend,' Garth corrected. 'You

. . . you have heard the news, I suppose?'

'Yes; I've just come in and Hilton told me. I — I still haven't got over the shock.' Hesitation. 'I'm just ready now to make the trip to Worthing. What I can't understand is what dad was doing there.'

'That, Miss Hammond, is only part of the puzzle,' Garth sighed. 'I shall want to ask you quite a lot of questions later. You have enough to do now in getting to Worthing and identifying the body. I'll be round to see you first thing in the morning . . . Oh, there's one thing you can perhaps tell me now.'

Garth reached on to the desk amidst the effects of Benson T. Hammond.

'I have a letter here, Miss Hammond,' Garth resumed. 'It had been torn up and then stuck together again. I'd like your views on it . . . ' He read it out deliberately and then asked: 'Well?'

'I'm not really surprised to learn that it was in dad's wallet,' Claire responded. 'I tore it up and threw it in the wastepaper basket in my bedroom. When I got home I found that it had gone. I guessed dad was responsible.'

'Then the note *was* sent to you?' Garth questioned. 'By Harvey Dell?'

'So I believed. I've seen Harvey since, though, and he denied that he had ever sent it.'

'He did, eh?' Garth muttered. 'Did you keep the appointment as he asked?'

'I *tried* to. I saw a manservant who said I had made a mistake, then the door was slammed in my face. I went straight to Harvey's flat to ask him about it and he was out. I waited until quarter to ten for him to arrive, and then he denied he had ever sent the letter. I think he *did* send it — and that he's hiding something. I'm certain it is his writing because it tallies with some other letters of which I have.'

'That,' Garth said, 'is interesting. I'll pick one of those letters up in the morning, and I'll have our experts check this note we have here. We'll soon find out if it's a forgery . . . Anyway, I shan't need to ask you any more over the phone, Miss Hammond. See you in the morning. Goodbye.'

Garth put the telephone down and

pulling out a leather case, selected a cheroot. 'The major problem is how Hammond got from London to here in the space of ten minutes. It means that he traveled from London to here at about three hundred and sixty miles an hour! By road he obviously couldn't do it.'

'Aeroplane?' Whittaker suggested, thinking. 'That would explain Hammond's crack on the skull and his peculiar flaccid bone condition.'

'It's the only answer,' Inspector Grimshaw insisted, who by this time was in possession of all the facts concerning the mysterious house in Stanton Street. 'According to Dr. Tenworthy's report, Hammond suffered from a disease of the bones — *ossium* something — that made his bones as brittle as glass. Very well then — if he were dropped from an aeroplane flying at a great height it would produce exactly the effect we found. Shattered bones . . . '

'Impossible,' Garth growled. 'I tell you that Hammond went into that house and couldn't get out without being seen. Even if he had — how do you imagine he was removed to an airfield? The nearest to Stanton Street is several miles distant. An aeroplane can't casually take off in the middle of London.'

'A helicopter can,' Whittaker pointed out. 'If perhaps it were on that condemned site opposite, the boarding hiding it from the street . . . ' He stopped and sighed. 'Won't do. It still doesn't explain how Hammond got to it — or was taken to it.'

'And I've yet to see the helicopter which can move at three-sixty miles an hour in the midst of fog and drizzle on a November night,' Garth retorted. 'And why should anybody *want* to drop the body on the Worthing road? Any road would have done if the idea was to suggest multiple injuries from being run over . . . '

'What about his head injury?' Grimshaw asked. 'Do you suppose somebody hit him with a blunt instrument?'

'Damned if I know,' Garth growled. 'Everything seems to start with Harvey Dell, though he seems to have been out of the picture at the time this mysterious business happened. But there's something odd about his denying writing that letter. And he knows where nine Stanton Street is because he was trailed there last night by Billings and Cassell . . . Yes, I think we'll start with him.'

Garth glanced at Grimshaw. 'Dr. Tenworthy's making a post-mortem of the body tonight. Ask him to send his report to me. This business is mine, but I'll keep in touch with you. Wrap up those effects belonging to Hammond and I'll take them with me. Tomorrow as soon as it's light, I want you and the best men you've got to make a thorough search of the road and surrounding district where Morton said he found the body. Let me have a report.'

Grimshaw gave a nod and handed over Hammond's effects when he had put them in an envelope and sealed it. Whittaker took it.

'That's all for now,' Garth said. 'Have us driven to the station and we'll get the next train for London.'

Harvey Dell opened one eye and contemplated an almost dark bedroom. The curtains were still drawn. It seemed that the telephone had been ringing. He wondered if he had been dreaming — then the ringing came again, long and insistent, muffled somewhat by the closed bedroom door. It was the bell on the flat's main door.

Harvey switched on the bedside light. His watch read one-ten. Muttering to himself at the disturbance, he drew on a dressing gown, pushed his feet into slippers, and stumbled sleepily through the lounge. Opening the main door, he beheld two men standing outside it, the one square and powerfully built with ice-blue eyes; the other very tall and stiff backed with a heavy neck.

'Mr. Harvey Dell?' inquired the shorter one.

'Yes, I'm he,' Harvey agreed, pushing back his disheveled hair.

'Sorry to disturb you at this hour, sir. I'm Inspector Garth of the C.I.D.; this is Sergeant Whittaker . . . ' Garth displayed his warrant card.

'Oh? Well — come in . . . ' Harvey motioned into the lounge and closed the door. He nodded to chairs. Garth sat down and took off his hat. Whittaker drifted to a chair near the table and brought out his notebook.

'Cigarettes?' Harvey inquired, holding out a box — but Garth shook his head. It almost seemed as though Harvey were trying to gain time in which to straighten out his thoughts.

'I understand, sir,' Garth said quietly, 'that you are a close friend of Miss Claire Hammond?'

'Yes, I am — we're as good as engaged.' Harvey frowned after he had lighted his cigarette. 'But what the devil has that got to do with Scotland Yard?' he asked sharply. 'Nothing's happened to Claire, has it?'

'No. But her father is dead, and in circumstances so unusual that police inquiry is necessary.'

'*Dead?* Good God! You mean stabbed, shot, or something?'

'At the moment we are not exactly sure how Mr. Hammond met his death.'

Garth's pale eyes never left Harvey's face. 'However, since you'll read the details in the newspapers soon enough you may as well know the facts. Mr. Hammond's body was found this evening about ten to eight on the Shoreham-Worthing coast road. Every bone in his body was broken, his skull was fractured, and there was enough dirt on his clothes to suggest that he had been run over several times.'

'But — how ghastly!' Harvey breathed, staring.

'At twenty to eight, sir,' Garth continued, 'Mr. Hammond entered number nine Stanton Street — in London here. He did not leave that house by any known material means — yet ten minutes later his body was found on the Worthing road sixty miles away.'

Harvey frowned. 'That's impossible. Fantastic!'

'Maybe — but those are the facts, and I've got to discover how such an incredible state of affairs came about. For that reason I have begun my investigation.'

'Here? Surely you don't suppose that I

mysteriously wafted Mr. Hammond's body to the Worthing road, do you?'

'I wouldn't be such a fool as to say that, Mr. Dell. All I am asking for is your co-operation. I got your address from a . . . letter.'

'What do you want to know?' Harvey asked.

'I want to know, sir, what connection you have with number nine Stanton Street.'

'So that's it! Since you mentioned a letter that means you have been talking to Claire — Miss Hammond.'

'Yes, I have,' Garth admitted, 'but that is immaterial. You sent a letter asking her to meet you at nine Stanton Street: when she got there all knowledge of you was denied.'

'She imagined everything,' Harvey retorted. 'I never wrote such a letter. And since she's destroyed it — so she says — it can't be proved.'

'But it can,' the chief inspector said imperturbably. 'I have it amongst Mr. Hammond's effects.

'Apparently,' Garth proceeded, as Harvey

remained silent, 'Miss Hammond tore the letter up and her father pieced it together again, putting it in his wallet. The letter says that you asked Miss Hammond to destroy it, in case her father should read it. Evidently he did. Then he went to number nine Stanton Street to find his daughter — After that, I don't know what *did* happen. The fact remains that, denial to Miss Hammond or otherwise you *have* a connection with that Stanton Street house and I'd like you to tell me what it is.'

'But I haven't!' Harvey insisted.

Garth's expression changed. The vaguely genial look faded and his face became as rigid as a death mask. 'You're not being very helpful, are you? Last night two plainclothes men followed you in your car from Hammond's home to nine Stanton Street. And it *was* you they followed. Denying all connection with the place won't do you a scrap of good.'

Harvey's face darkened with anger. 'What the devil were two plainclothes men doing following me?'

'For your information, Mr. Dell, Mr. Hammond asked for protection from a mysterious writer of threatening messages. Two men were detailed to keep a check on Hammond and callers. You happened to be a caller and you were followed . . . Now, what can you tell me about that Stanton Street house?'

'Nothing!' Harvey retorted. 'I never heard such a cock-and bull story in my life.'

'And do you also deny that you sent that letter to Miss Hammond?'

'Most emphatically! That letter is a forgery.'

'Our calligraphy department will soon decide that,' Garth responded. 'The letter will be compared tomorrow with one of the letters you sent Miss Hammond at an earlier date. Why not help me, and yourself — '

'I've nothing to say!' Harvey said flatly.

Garth got to his feet, his face still grim. 'What were your relations towards Mr. Hammond, Mr. Dell?'

Harvey shrugged. 'I don't see any reason for hiding the fact that I quarrelled with Mr. Hammond on Monday night.'

'Quarrelled . . . About what?'

'My becoming engaged to Miss Hammond. I asked her father's permission and he ordered me out of the house. I — I think he got the impression that I was on the hunt for money far more than Claire's hand. I had no choice but to leave. But I promised Claire that I would write to her.'

'And so you sent her that letter arranging to meet her at Stanton Street instead of this flat?'

'No.' Harvey shook his head. 'In the finish I didn't write to her at all.'

Garth said: 'Perhaps you can help me in another way . . . Can you give me an account of your movements tonight — *last* night to be strictly accurate — from six o'clock onwards?'

'I think so.' Harvey assented. 'At about quarter past six I left the N.T.C. — that's the place where I work, the National Teleradio Combine — on the outskirts of London, out Cricklewood way. I'm a senior electronic engineer.' He smiled faintly. 'I have been referred to as a boffin.'

'Mmmm. I understand. And then?'

'I drove my car into the city centre, had some tea, and then dropped in at the Science Club in Albemarle Street for an hour. I had some important reference work to look up. I'm a member of the Science Club, you see.'

'And you left the Club at — ?'

'Oh, about a quarter past eight.'

'Anybody see you enter or leave the club? Is there anybody who can verify your statement?'

'No.' Harvey gave a troubled frown. 'That's the awkward part. But it's true.'

'If you say so.' Garth reflected for a moment. 'Then what did you do? Come on here?'

'Not at first. Believe it or not, I do most of my thinking when I'm driving around in my car. I did just that — until a quarter to ten. Then I came here and to my amazement found Miss Hammond waiting for me. She told me all about that phony letter she had received and . . . Well, that's all there is,' he finished, tightening the sash about his dressing gown.

'Pity you've no witnesses,' Garth said dryly. 'If there's nothing else you can tell me I'll be on my way, with apologies once again for this late call. I'll get in touch with you if I need to. Ready, Sergeant?'

Whittaker nodded and thrust his notebook in his pocket. He and Garth were in the self-service lift before he made a comment.

'What do you make of Dell, sir?'

Garth smiled grimly. 'I think he's about the most consummate liar I've ever come across. How much of a liar he is I can't say until we've looked a bit further.'

'Then what's next, sir?'

'Right now,' Garth said, stepping out of the lift into the wide hall with its subdued lighting, 'I'm going home to bed. Hammond can't become any deader than he is, and I'm no superman. We'll pick up the threads again in the daylight.'

5

Garth entered his office at nine the following morning. He looked grey-faced and bad-tempered and apparently had not profited much from the few hours' sleep he had managed.

'Getting me down, Whitty, is this business,' he declared, settling in the swivel chair. 'It's impossible!'

Whittaker motioned to the blotter where he had arranged various reports and correspondence in orderly series.

'Everything's there, sir,' he commented. 'Some pretty interesting — if not creepy — facts, too.'

Garth picked up the first report. It was from Dr. Tenworthy, his post-mortem on Hammond's body complete. The notch between Garth's eyebrows deepened as he read:

★ ★ ★

Post-mortem Report on Benson Thomas Hammond Dec'd:

Cause of death I ascribe to multiple injuries, or to severe blow on the skull resulting in a compound fracture. This fracture seems to have been caused by some kind of weapon of the type of a poker or iron bar and apparently was used with extreme force. The alternative suggestion is that the blow itself was not so savage but that the condition of the victim's bone structure was so fragile that the impact created a fracture that would only have bruised a man with normal bone development.

The deceased suffered from 'fragilitas ossiumtarda', a disease embracing calcification of the bones. This, however, could not account for the total destruction of every bone in his body.

X-ray plates, herewith, reveal that not a single bone is intact. All the bones are reduced to fragments, the fragments being loosely connected by tissue and cartilage. Assuming that the deceased was run over several times, and taking into account the disease from which he suffered, I consider it extremely unlikely that every bone in his body would be broken in this manner.

Further, there is the strange maladjustment of some of the internal organs (see plates herewith). It will be noted that the caecum is in the position usually occupied by the liver, whilst the liver is where the caecum should be, Also, the appendix is in the position where the small intestine usually lies. Yet there is no sign of anatomical disturbance in the transference (i.e. the change in positions having been accomplished by crushing).

It would appear that the deceased's internal organs were always arranged in this fashion, yet if this was the case I cannot understand as a medical man, how he lived an apparently healthy life and never complained of severe internal pain.

* * *

'In fact,' Garth commented, putting the report down and sighing, 'Hammond seems to have been in one hell of a mess!'

'I'm wondering sir, if we should ring up the L.C.C. — or go to their offices — and get a map of the sewers in the Stanton Street area?'

'Yes, it's a good idea,' Garth agreed, 'even though the water at the bottom of that shaft in number nine Stanton Street isn't a sewer: it has no smell. Just the same, all details about it are what we need . . . No news from those two relief men at number nine, I suppose?'

'No *good* news, sir. They've reported that nothing's happened.'

'And no information on the writer of those threats?'

'Nothing, sir.'

Garth got to his feet and from his overcoat took out a morning paper. He tossed it on the desk. 'Read this?'

Whittaker nodded but he looked again.

MILLIONAIRE SHIPPER'S
MYSTERY TRANSITION

'Mr. Benson T. Hammond, the well-known millionaire Maida Vale shipowner, founder of the Hammond

Freight Shipping Line, was found dead last night on the Brighton-Worthing coast road. The possibility of foul play is not ruled out and the police are making inquiries. Scotland Yard has been called in. A puzzling feature of Mr. Hammond's death is that witnesses assert that he entered a London house at 7-40 last night, ten minutes before he was discovered by Mr. Andrew Morton, a commercial traveler, on the Worthing road.'

'Who do you suppose handed out this information?' Whittaker asked.

'Maybe Grimshaw: maybe a snooping reporter — might even have been Miss Hammond herself. Can't suppress news of this sort, Whitty ... And with the business exposed to the glare of day like this we've got to do something — Let's start by having a word with Miss Hammond.'

Towards quarter to ten they were being admitted into the lounge of the Hammond home. Claire Hammond came in to them presently, pale, troubled, the wear and tear of a sleepless night ill-concealed by a liberal use of cosmetics.

'Miss Hammond . . . ' Garth greeted her quietly as he shook hands. 'And Detective-sergeant Whittaker.'

'Please sit down, gentlemen.' Claire motioned to chairs and then settled on the chesterfield. 'I — I managed to identify my father . . . It was a horrible task. Horrible!'

'I'm sure it must have been,' Garth conceded, with unusual gentleness. 'At a time like this, I don't at all like having to ask you questions . . . But it must be done.'

'I understand.' Claire nodded quickly. 'I'm over the worst of the shock now. I've had a terrible sleepless night, though — and then the journeying back and forth. To lose your father and your intended fiancé all in one swoop is pretty staggering.'

'You mean Mr. Dell, I suppose?' Garth asked.

'Yes — Harvey Dell. After the — well, after the lies he told me last night I just couldn't keep up the pretence of wanting to be engaged to him. I think my father guessed right in saying that Harvey's not straight.'

'I saw Mr. Dell early this morning,' Garth said. 'He told me that he had quarrelled with your father. Is that true?'

'Quite true,' Claire responded. 'On Monday evening Harvey went into Dad's study to ask if we might announce our engagement. Father told me he'd agreed at first, then retracted his consent when Harvey asked him for two million pounds to finance some 'high-flown' notion. It struck him as being the act of a rabid fortune-hunter, and I must say that I can see his point of view now, though I couldn't at the time.'

'A high-flown notion . . . ' Garth mused. 'Know what he meant by that?'

'Sorry,' Claire sighed. 'Harvey certainly never mentioned anything 'high-flown' to me — Oh, I do remember something! While the interview was going on I sat on the stairs to wait. Now and again I could hear Dad and Harvey arguing, but it wasn't about me — as I'd expected. It seemed to be about business.'

'Try to remember the exact words, Miss Hammond,' Garth said earnestly

'First of all, Dad said something to the effect that he 'wouldn't hear of it'. And then Harvey said — ' . . . a chance to beat the airlines at their own games if you' — meaning Daddy — 'weren't so hidebound'. I think Dad then said something about 'damned rubbish' and Harvey's response was a reference to 'cuts in shipping rates' and something about 'distance'. After that Harvey came out of the study and Dad ordered him to leave and never come back. Harvey went, promising to get in touch with me by letter.'

'Then you received this letter from Mr. Dell?' Garth asked, and from his wallet handed over the patched missive.

Claire glanced at it and nodded. From a concealed pocket in her dress she handed over another letter in its envelope. 'This is one of Mr. Dell's earlier letters to me, Mr. Garth,' she explained. 'It's one of the — less amorous letters.'

'Have no fear, Miss Hammond. We'll respect your confidence in helping us in this fashion. We're only interested in the handwriting.' He studied the two letters together and raised his eyebrows. 'Mmmm — same notepaper, same watermark and apparently the same handwriting. *And* the same embossed heading . . . I think Mr. Dell is a singularly foolish young man to deny that he sent you this latest letter.'

Claire looked serious. 'Then he denied it to you as well?'

Garth nodded and put the letters away in his wallet. 'What did he say to you, Miss Hammond? When did you see him?'

'About a quarter to ten last night. I'd been waiting for him for quite some time. You will remember that I told you over the phone that I went straight to question him after I'd made that fool's errand to Stanton Street.'

'And you tackled Mr. Dell the moment you saw him?'

'I was going to, but the telephone prevented me. It had been ringing in Harvey's flat most of the evening. It started again just when he arrived. I said I wanted an explanation for the note and he said he'd tell me all about it when he'd answered the phone. But he denied he had ever sent the note, told me I had been dreaming, and . . . ' Claire sighed. 'I walked out on him. Any girl worth her salt would have done the same.'

Garth said: 'Miss Hammond, I would like to be absolutely certain . . . You say that Mr. Dell said he would tell you all about it? You mean about the letter?'

'Yes. He as good as admitted that he'd sent it. I got the impression that he was quite willing to explain — and that he afterwards changed his mind.'

'After answering the telephone?' Garth prompted.

'Why, yes! His mood changed quite a lot after he had answered that call. I remember his expression too — sort of interested, then amazed and finally pretty nearly horrified. I didn't attach much importance to it at the time.'

'You don't know who telephoned, I suppose?'

'No. I was standing by the door and didn't get a single word through the receiver.'

'Can you remember what Mr. Dell said?'

'A little. Something about 'He did?' — asking a question about somebody. Then he said: 'You *did!*' presumably to the person speaking. After that he seemed to have quite a shock for he looked horrified and gasped 'Good heavens!' He finished up with something about leaving him to think it out.'

'All very interesting,' Garth said, and his fixed expression relaxed into a genial smile. 'Tell me, Miss Hammond, has Mr. Dell any friends or acquaintances you know of?'

'Quite a few, but there are only two of whom I've heard anything definite. One of them is Clifton Brand — pretty wealthy chap who has a dress salon in Regent Street. The other is Leslie Carson. He's an employee of the Noonhill Teleradio Company, where — in case you don't know — Harvey is also employed.'

'Thanks,' Garth acknowledged. 'The information may be helpful. Yes, I know about Mr. Dell's occupation. I understand he is an electronic engineer . . . '

A profound thought seemed to pervade Garth for a moment, then his attention centred on the girl again.

'Last evening you saw Mr. Dell at nine-forty-five, which checks with his statement to me. And of course you had not seen him at any time before that — since he left this house the night before?'

'But I did!' Claire said quickly. 'At least I think so. I saw his car in Stanton Street. He might have been driving it.'

'What time?' Garth asked sharply.

Claire gave a résumé of the incident in detail and it left the chief inspector with the death mask back on his face. He rubbed his chest gently as it gave a dyspeptic twinge.

'When you went into that house in Stanton Street last night, Miss Hammond, whom did you see? Can you describe exactly what you did?'

'I rang the bell and knocked. Getting no immediate answer, I tried to peep in at the front windows. There were curtains over them and a pink light behind. I remember I found myself standing on a sort of grid and I peeped below to see if there were any lights. I guessed that there was a cellar there — '

'And you couldn't see anything?'

'No. Everything was totally dark. Then somebody's voice startled me and I saw a man in the portico — '

'Was there a light in the hall?'

'A dim one,' Claire assented. 'I couldn't see the man's face properly . . . He stood just inside the hall with the dim light shining down on him. I remember thinking that his forehead, cheekbones, and chin made sort of white spots where the light caught them, and the rest of his face was in shadow . . . I could dimly see that he had a frockcoat and once as he moved he gave me a glimpse of striped trousers. No doubt that he was a manservant all right — Oh yes, I remember he was extremely tall.'

'And he told you that you had made a mistake in going to that house?'

'Most emphatically. I told him whom I was, why I had come, but it made no difference. He just shut the door on me.'

Garth frowned. 'When you tried to

look into that cellar and couldn't see anything, could you *hear* anything?'

'Not that I recall. In fact I remember thinking how dreadfully quiet everything was.'

'Mr. Dell's two friends — Mr. Brand and Mr. Carson. Have you ever met them? Can you describe them?'

'I never met them,' Claire responded. 'I've only heard Harvey speak of them.' The girl made a restless movement. 'My poor father! I'm convinced that he must have followed me — '

'He did,' Garth interrupted. 'We know that much. I think you should know that he appealed to me for protection against a threatening letter-writer.'

Claire looked surprised. 'He never mentioned it to me.'

'Hardly. No man likes to appear scared in front of his own daughter. However, we had plainclothes men keeping guard over him. They saw him go into number nine Stanton Street, but they never saw him come out. Ten minutes after he went into the house he was found in Worthing by a commercial traveler — as by now you must know.'

Claire looked completely blank. Garth gave a troubled smile. 'Yes,' he said, 'it sounds fantastic! Yet it happened.'

'I was told by the Worthing inspector about that commercial traveler finding Dad,' the girl said. 'I suppose it was on your orders that Simmons, the chauffeur, refrained from telling me anything when I questioned him?'

'Yes. At the time I didn't know properly how things stood and I asked him to keep quiet, rather than have him mix things up.'

'I . . . see.' Claire wrestled with the impossible situation, then: 'So what happens now?'

'A great deal,' Garth answered. 'The amazing fact that your father was found sixty miles distant ten minutes after being seen in London is not the only problem. There is the equally baffling problem of number nine Stanton Street itself . . . ' Sketchily he outlined the circumstances and the effect was to make Claire sit back limply in her chair.

'Sounds like fantasy,' Garth went on.

'But as somebody once remarked, there is a grain of scientific truth in every breath of fantasy ... I'm wondering about the possibility of a twin. Had your father a brother?'

Claire shook her head. 'No. You can dismiss any doubts about it being Father. I'd know him anywhere.'

'Have you anything in the house which he handled a good deal, Miss Hammond?'

'To check fingerprints, you mean? Yes — there's a paperknife in his study that he used constantly. I'll get it — '

'It'll do as I leave, thanks,' Garth interrupted. 'There's something else — have you the name of your father's physician?'

'He had two,' Claire responded. 'One is the family doctor — Dr. Blair, who attends to me as well; then there is Sir Wilson Barnett, the osteopath. Father paid him frequent visits on account of a bone disease he had.'

'You knew about that, then?'

Claire nodded. 'When I was a child he was frightened lest I might have inherited it. Apparently I have not. It was the one thing in life that he feared because up to being a man he was bedridden and he was terrified of ever having to go back to that again. Apparently, when he matured, the disease became less severe and he started work, married, and finished up as a shipping magnate. My father,' Claire finished, with a wistful smile, 'was a very persevering, determined man.'

'Did anybody else know of his disease?' Garth inquired.

'I expect so. He made no attempt to keep it a secret: he hardly could. He had to explain to most people why he liked gentle handshakes, avoided sports, sat down carefully and such things as that . . . '

'Did Harvey Dell know?' Claire nodded.

Garth rose. 'Well, Miss Hammond, I'm sorry I had to bother you with so many routine questions. There'll be an inquest in Worthing, of course, which you will be asked to attend. I'll secure an adjournment until our investigation's finished and some conclusion as to the cause of death reached.'

'And I presume Daddy can be . . . buried?'

'That is up to the Worthing coroner. I see no reason why he should withhold permission now the body has been identified and he himself has viewed it.'

Claire stood up. 'Mr. Garth, tell me something. Do you believe Dad was murdered?'

'At the moment, Miss Hammond, I'm in no position to say anything, either one way or the other. I wish I were. The moment I do know something definite I'll acquaint you . . . Now I'd better have that paperknife.'

6

Towards mid morning Garth and Whittaker returned to their office at the Yard. The paperknife was duly handed over to 'Dabs' with instructions to check the prints on it with those of the corpse.

Garth threw himself into the swivel chair, rubbed his chest, and gave a gentle belch. He looked at Whittaker, seated at his own desk and leafing through his notebook pages relevant to the case so far.

'Let's see what we've got so far,' Garth suggested. 'First, to the kingpin in the whole business — Harvey Dell. We both think he is a liar? Any idea why?'

'I've two suggestions, sir. One: that revealing his real activities might make him look like Hammond's murderer, if murdered he was — or Two: he actually did murder him and so is trying to make things tough for us.'

'There's a third possibility,' Garth lit a

cheroot. 'That Dell is shielding somebody and getting deeper in the mess every minute in trying to do it. As a random shot let's say the person who rang him up. From the moment Dell got that phone message he about-turned in his tracks. Otherwise he would have taken far more care in concealing his earlier movements. Miss Hammond even saw his car — and I'll bet he was driving it — leaving number nine Stanton Street . . . Where Dell went we don't know yet because he is evading telling the truth.

'We also know that he was willing to explain about that note had not that telephone message stopped him. From then on he turned into a stubborn liar, even to the extent of losing the girl he purports to love. And according to Miss Hammond, he was amazed and then horrified by what he heard over the wire.'

'Suggesting that he did send that letter?'

'I'm sure of it, and our experts should verify it.' Garth took the two letters from his wallet. 'Take them along, Whitty, and let's be having the answer.

Tell 'em to hurry it up.'

When Whittaker returned he found Garth brooding amidst a haze of cheroot smoke.

'We also know,' he went on, as though there had been no break, 'that Dell visited Stanton Street on Monday night, which is proof positive that he's connected with that house. Yes, he's the kingpin all right, but I don't know at this stage whether he is the culprit. In spite of his lies I rather like the man.'

'Wouldn't it be possible to trace through the Exchange who telephoned to him?' Whittaker asked.

'I don't think so. I noticed that Dell has a dial telephone. Further, anybody with a serious message — secret message if you prefer — would not risk an Exchange listening in, so the call probably came from an automatic callbox — untraceable.'

Garth went over to the steel locker cupboard on the opposite side of the office, and mixed himself a drink, downed it, rumbled and considered the view through the window.

'Let's narrow the field,' he resumed. 'Miss Hammond referred to those two friends of Dell's — Brand and Carson. It might have been either on the phone. No harm in inquiring, anyway. Whoever telephoned knows the answer to all this — As does Harvey Dell of course, but he's determined to keep it to himself.'

'The others probably won't speak either,' Whittaker pointed out.

'We have to try,' Garth growled. 'Meantime we have only our own precious theories to rely on ... Let's consider number nine Stanton Street first. How do you account for that deserted spooks' den with the dust everywhere?'

'I thought a good deal about that last night, sir. Ruling out the 'impossible' as the answer, I then considered the *possible* angles. I also referred to Hans Gross's section on dust and satisfied myself that dust is usually, One: Brought about by wind; Two: Created by people within the house; or Three: It filters through cracks. My mind wandered to that planking across the basement window — apparently a fairly recent job — and I asked myself if it was possible for so *much* dust to have fallen in a house which, to judge from that boarding, had not been deserted for more than a few months. How did the dust *get* there? The windows are sealed up; the drain-shaft with water at the bottom couldn't carry dust — So, from where?'

Garth grinned round his cheroot. 'I believe I'll make a copper out of you yet, Whitty! And your final conclusion?'

'The dust was deliberately put there — but the culprit rather overdid it — there was enough dust on those floors to sow spuds in.' Whittaker paused. 'There have been plenty of cases where dust has been added after the crime, sir, to confuse the police. It's done with a fine sieve, a bag like that on a vacuum cleaner, and a bellows handle. Press the bellows handle back and forth and dust shoots out of the sieve on the end of a nozzle. A vacuum-cleaner in reverse.'

'Exactly right,' Garth agreed, beaming. 'On that theory, Whitty, we both agree.

The dust *was* produced afterwards. It was still hazy and unsettled in the air when we were looking the place over. Reason? To suggest that the place had never been entered for long enough. And what became of the person who laid the dust?'

'Well, sir, I could imagine that he went down that shaft and took the dust-bellows with him, but then I recall there was undisturbed dust on the grid itself and the grid is locked from underneath. On that,' Whittaker confessed, frowning, 'I'm sunk for the moment. That's why I suggested we get a map of the sewers or something and try and figure it out from below instead of from above.'

'And we will! Later on.' Garth rubbed his hands together. 'All right, we've solved the dust problem. How about the vanishing curtains and lighting?'

'According to accounts the lighting was really dim. That suggested to me a low source of power. Perhaps a battery — or batteries in series — somewhere, lighting both hall and front room and maybe the cellar. That would explain away the sealed utility meters for there would be no need to use them. To clear away a battery-driven lighting set, the wires probably only slung up carelessly, would not take five minutes. Result — no sign of where the light came from. Always assuming, sir,' Whittaker finished seriously, 'that that shaft is the answer to where all the tackle went — *and* the perpetrator thereof.'

'And the curtains?'

Whittaker shrugged. 'We don't know that they were screwed to the window frame. They could have been fastened on to a separate framework on the clothes-horse principle, so arranged that each window was covered. Once the light was out the windows were so grimy that the removal of the curtains would not be noticed from outside on a dark, drizzling night such as it was. Then the dust was laid. Maybe a masked torch was used to watch the effect. It would not be seen from outside but it would satisfy the 'operator' as to whether or not he was doing his job properly.'

'And like the rest of the stuff the curtains and hypothetical framework went down the shaft?' Garth murmured.

'It's just a theory, sir,' Whittaker apologized, looking under his eyes.

'Theory be damned, man! If we're not to believe in fairies it's the only answer! You've done a nice piece of work, my lad. There's only one pity about it all ... *Why*? And what the devil was that house used for, I wonder?' Garth muttered. 'I admit the hoary old idea of counterfeiters had occurred to me. I thought of presses or something like that, stuff that could be quickly taken apart and thrown down the shaft ... But Miss Hammond heard no sounds whatever, and there is no power laid on. You'd need it to run a modern counterfeiting press. Batteries wouldn't suffice.'

Garth stubbed his cheroot. 'I'm leaving the house's *purpose* as a question mark for now. The answer will probably be in the mud of the water at the base of that shaft — and that is where we've got to go before long, once we've traced how to get to the damned thing ... Second problem is why — and how — was Hammond killed? And, glory be, how did he do his famous three hundred and sixty mile an hour act?'

'Nothing clicks on the last part, sir,' Whittaker said. 'As to motive — well, both Harvey Dell and Miss Hammond had a good one, don't you think?

'Not really strong enough,' Garth said flatly. 'I just can't picture the girl wishing to murder her father because he refused to consent to the engagement. She could walk out and get married anyway . . . it doesn't fit.'

'She will probably inherit the Hammond millions,' Whittaker pointed out. '*That* fits! So far we have only Miss Hammond's word for it for everything she has done, and for where she went last night. We don't *know* that she went to Stanton Street — '

'But we do know that she described the place accurately. No, Whitty, it still doesn't fit . . . As for Harvey Dell, well, there we *might* have something. He had more than just a rejected engagement to avenge: there was something else — that business talk and the request for two million pounds . . . Mmmm. With old man Hammond dead Claire as you say, will probably inherit the money and she might help Dell, or at least was inclined to until he about-faced. But that in its turn, makes a mess of the theory that it is the person who telephoned who is the central figure — Hell!' Garth finished in disgust.

Long interval during which Whittaker looked through his notes. Then:

'Y'know, Whitty, I've got another idea batting about in my brain. Last night when we interviewed Dell he said he works as a senior electronic engineer at the Noonhill Teleradio Combine. The idea died out and then came back again when Miss Hammond mentioned it too — Senior electronic engineer. That's no ordinary job.'

'No, sir; it's a highly technical one,' Whittaker said, and Garth jerked up an eyebrow.

'I read the *American Science Monthly* a lot, and the *Scientific American*. Thinking of getting 'em bound when I can get round to it. A Stateside cousin of mine sends 'em — '

'What in hell are you rambling about?'

Garth asked heavily.

'Sorry, sir. Electronic engineer. Highly skilled job. Electronics are — or is — an outgrowth of atomic science. I don't know exactly what the science embraces but roundly I'd say it is the technique of forces and their makeup. Unfortunately,' Whittaker sighed, 'I'm no scientist.'

'No, neither am I,' Garth responded. 'And I begin to think that in these modern days we *should* be. Criminals and science have been going hand in hand these last few years . . . '

Whittaker asked hesitantly: 'What, sir, was the idea you had batting around?'

'Eh? Oh yes! Well, connecting Dell's profession of electronic engineer with his . . . ' Garth swung round irritably at a knock on the door. 'Come in!' he snapped.

A sergeant appeared. 'There's a Miss Barrow here, sir,' he said. 'She says she has some information she wishes to give you concerning the Hammond business, so I thought — '

'Okay.' Garth nodded and stood up. His eyes travelled over the austere-looking woman in the mid-forties who came into the office. She had frosty grey eyes, a school-ma'am hairdo, and was wearing a severely tailored tweed costume.

'Good morning, madam.' Garth took her somewhat unresponsive hand and motioned to the chair Whittaker had vacated. 'Have a chair, will you? This is Detective-sergeant Whittaker.'

Whittaker nodded and silently wished the woman to the devil.

'Now Miss Barrow . . . ' Garth returned to his swivel chair. 'You have some information concerning the late Mr. Hammond, I believe?'

'Yes.' The woman paused, moistened her lips quickly, and then said: 'I am, or rather was, Mr. Hammond's personal secretary. I occupied that position for thirty years.'

The woman ducked her head and began a quick searching through her handbag. Finally she produced a copy of a morning paper and pointed a finger at it significantly,

'This was the first intimation I received of Mr. Hammond's terrible, not to say mysterious fate,' she explained. 'Since I did not get a chance to read the paper until late this morning, I hadn't the facts any sooner. As soon as I had, I came here.'

The chief inspector shifted position. 'You came here — about what?'

'Mr. Hammond came to you about some mysterious threatening notes he had been receiving, didn't he? I know he said he was going to.'

'Yes, he did.' Garth's pale eyes sharpened. 'What about it?'

'The problem to him was how on earth those notes ever got into the mail, presumably through the mail box, without the night watchman ever seeing the deliverer.'

'If it can be called a problem, yes,' Garth admitted. 'I have men busy investigating and — '

'Then you had better recall them.' A vague cloud of triumph seemed to hover about the plain-faced, extremely spinster-ish Miss Barrow. 'The explanation of how the notes got into the mail is absurdly simple . . . *I* put them there.'

Garth kept his features impassive.

'I cut the messages out of newspapers, pasted them on cheap notepaper, put them in cheap envelopes, and handed them to Mr. Hammond with his mail at regular intervals. Naturally I hadn't the least intention of carrying out the threats the notes contained. In fact they hardly *were* threats.'

'Then why the devil did you send them?' Garth demanded.

'I wanted,' Miss Barrow replied, gazing serenely at him with her bleak eyes, 'to make him squirm. No more, no less. And he *did* squirm! I don't think I ever saw a man so frightened.'

'And why did you desire to make him squirm?' Garth asked, staring at her somewhat blankly.

'Because he was a swine to work for. In all the time I worked for him he never had a good word for me. At one time I nearly left him and he doubled my salary to make me stay on. Another time I was leaving to get married — some fifteen years ago — but by some machination which I never solved Mr. Hammond poisoned my fiancé's mind against me and I was back where I started — serving Hammond. Because of him I have become what I am now — a frozen-faced old maid whom no man in his right senses would look at twice! Under his dictates I threw away my youth, my chances, everything. I only realized that when it was too late. *That* is why I wanted to make him uncomfortable in the way safest to myself.'

Garth cleared his throat. 'I don't think I ever heard a woman make a confession so . . . baldly.'

Miss Barrow gave a faint, wintry smile. 'I had intended to send them for years if need be, and so make Hammond live in perpetual fear. I knew he would, you see, because of a bone disease he had. He was terrified of being beaten up or anything like that. I became, without him once suspecting, his Grand Inquisitress . . . Then I saw about his death,' the woman continued, her mood changing, 'and I realized that my fun-and-games had got to stop immediately.'

'Very wise of you,' Garth agreed.

'I assure you, Inspector, that I had nothing to do with his death, or his visit to Worthing. Nothing!'

'You can help corroborate that statement, Miss Barrow, by giving an account of your movements yesterday evening from the time you left the office.'

The woman looked relieved. 'That's quite easy. I left the office with our head cashier, Mr. Podbury. He walked with me as far as the Women's Political Institute — I'm a strong Liberal supporter, you know — and I spent the evening at the Institute discussing politics with various friends of mine — '

'The address of the Institute, madam?' Garth interrupted.

'Calvin Road — not half a mile from the Hammond Building. As I was saying I spent the evening discussing politics. My various friends can all verify that. I left at nine-thirty and went home. I live with my married sister at 10 Vine Grove, Hammersmith. My sister — and her husband too — can verify that I was at home until I went to bed at eleven-forty-five.

Garth tossed down his pencil. 'Okay

then, Miss Barrow, and thanks for calling.'

The woman rose as he did. 'I am fully prepared, Inspector, to take whatever penalty is coming to me.'

'We shall have to go into that, madam, of course,' Garth said, opening the office door for her. 'I'll get in touch with you. Good morning.'

She went out with a half-puzzled look on her pale gray face and Garth closed the door gently. He turned and raised an eyebrow at Whittaker.

'That's one problem sorted out, anyway, sir,' he commented.

'Uh-huh . . . ' Garth chewed his cheroot pensively. 'Better tell Adams to check up on that alibi, Whitty. At the same time have those men recalled who are searching for the note-sender.'

Whittaker nodded and left the office. When he returned he found his superior still pondering at his desk.

'Is there a penalty for what Miss Barrow did, sir?'

'Since the notes didn't actually constitute a threat I don't think there is. There are other things more important to bother about . . . ' Garth twisted in the swivel chair as the telephone shrilled.

'Yes? Garth speaking . . . '

'Good morning, sir. Grimshaw here. Worthing police. I followed out your instructions and had a thorough search made of the immediate area where Hammond was found last evening. I had Andrew Morton point out the place and I supervised everything myself. There doesn't seem to be anything really definite. On one side of the road there is the sea and foreshore, and on the other there's more or less empty downland — except for a pretty large-sized Nissen hut.'

'Nissen hut?' Garth frowned slightly. 'You mean it is standing there all by itself? Doesn't it belong to somebody?'

'I'm instituting inquiries about it, sir. We found it padlocked and there's a small hand-made sign on the door saying 'Keep Out.' The windows have been blocked up with planking. We've no authority to break in so we're following routine methods. I can't see that the hut has any possible connection with Hammond — but since the hut is only a quarter of a mile from where the body was found I thought we'd better make sure. There's something else — From the hut there are clear sets of footprints. Remember how it drizzled last night and made the ground soft?'

'Go on,' Garth ordered, pondering.

'There are four sets of footprints in all — apparently all belonging to the same man. One set leads to the hut from the road; another very heavy set leads back to the road — then again there's a normal set from the road, and another back. It looks as though on one occasion something heavy was carried from the hut.'

'Man's prints?' Garth asked.

'Size nine, with steel horsehoes on the heels. Want me to make casts of them?'

'No, that isn't necessary — but find out who owns the hut and ask them to let you see inside it. If they won't you can get to the necessary authority. Go carefully: all this may be circumstantial and we can't afford to put our feet in it. Just the same that Nissen hut only a quarter of a mile from the body seems oddly coincidental to me. Besides, there is a peculiar parallel between the windows of that hut and the basement windows of the Stanton Street house.'

'Parallel, sir?' Grimshaw repeated.

'Both of them covered in boarding. Anyway, carry on, and let me know what you find.' Garth rang off and glanced up at Whittaker.

'I heard, sir,' Whittaker said. 'Hut or otherwise, though, it still doesn't explain how Hammond traveled sixty miles in ten minutes. And that reminds me!' Whittaker exclaimed, 'When Miss Barrow turned up you were going to explain a thought you'd had concerning Harvey Dell being an electronic engineer.'

'Oh — yes. Consider these three things, Whitty — First: Dell is an electronic engineer; Second: He argued with Hammond about freight charges, beating the airlines, cuts in shipping rates, and something about distance; and Third: He asked Hammond for money to finance something which Hammond called 'high-flown'. Mix them together and what do you get?'

Whittaker stared out of the office window upon the grey Thames Embankment. 'It looks,' he said, 'as though 'transit' has something to do with it. Beating the airlines and cutting shipping rates proves that point — so does the bit about 'distance'. But where that connects up with 'high-flown' I just can't imagine — unless 'high flown' has a slanting reference to electronics.'

Garth grinned round his cheroot. 'Course it has!' he declared. 'You're scientific, in a mild way — but if you were in Miss Hammond's or even in her father's position, knowing next to nothing about scientific things, wouldn't you consider anything involving electronics 'high-flown'?'

'That's right,' Whittaker admitted, surprised.

'If you can't explain a thing as being caused by supernatural means,' Garth continued, 'then the only other answer is *scientific* means. And that rears up the self-evident question mark of electronics.'

Silence. 'On top of that,' Garth

resumed, musing, 'consider this post-mortem report. Hammond's liver and caecum changed places! That too sounds impossible, but it isn't if what I have forming in my mind is correct — Er, you got the names of those two doctors of Hammond's, didn't you?'

Whittaker picked up his notebook. 'Dr. Blair's the family doctor, sir, and Sir Wilson Barnett is the osteopath.'

'Look 'em up in the directory. I expect Blair will be in the Maida Vale district. I want the addresses and then we'll have to go and see them. We can't prove our authority without a warrant card, and no doctor who knows his ethics would speak a word about a patient over the phone, to an apparently unauthorized stranger . . .'

Whittaker looked up the addresses, made a note of them, and then glanced up to see that Garth had got into his hat and coat and was putting the X-ray plates of Hammond's interior into a briefcase. Garth handed him the case. 'Ready?' he asked.

As Whittaker nodded, Garth added:

'I'd better leave word that any information reaching here concerning Miss Hammond, Dell, or even the Noonhill Teleradio Combine, must be relayed to me immediately. I can't afford to miss a single hint if I'm to get out of this mess with a whole skin . . . '

7

Professor Gordon Roberts, chief-of-staff of the research department of the Noonhill Teleradio Combine, walked swiftly down the long, spotless corridor that extended between his private office and the immense research laboratories.

He was a fiftyish man with wiry brown hair, bifocals, and a nose like a Roman centurion. His position in the Combine was highly responsible: practically all television research was encompassed in this Government-sponsored enterprise, hiding inside this immense one-floored edifice in Cricklewood, isolated from houses and district areas.

Professor Roberts entered the huge main research laboratory and looked about him. Endless scientific equipment and test and research benches were broken here and there by white-overalled men and women, engaged on all manner of experiments. One dark-haired man in particular, bending over a blueprint caught Roberts's attention. He approached him purposefully.

'Have you a moment, Mr. Dell?'

Harvey Dell glanced up from the blueprint and allowed it to roll up on itself. 'Something wrong, doctor?'

'I'm puzzled,' Dr. Roberts declared flatly. 'I've been trying all morning to locate Mr. Carson — without success'

'Oh? You mean Leslie Carson?'

'Naturally, man!' Roberts was irritable. 'We were to have had a consultation this morning concerning that new short-wave television circuit we're putting out, and I just can't find him anywhere. It's so unlike him.'

Harvey frowned. 'Yes, sir, it is,' he assented. 'I'd noticed that he was not about anywhere but I assumed he'd been assigned elsewhere in the building — '

'He isn't, and he doesn't seem to be at his lodgings, either. Look here, Dell, you and he are great friends. Have you no idea where he might be?'

'I'm afraid not,' Harvey said. 'I haven't seen him since he left here last evening.

He didn't mention he was going anywhere special: in fact he said he'd be seeing me this morning as usual . . . And you say he isn't at his rooms?'

'No.' Professor Roberts looked sombre. 'His landlady says he left his rooms about six-thirty last night saying he'd return about nine. He hasn't been seen since. I don't like it! He's one of the cleverest scientific engineers we have here, and apart from that he has secrets in his brain that would be worth any criminal's attention. Something,' Roberts finished grimly, 'may have happened to him. Since you, his best friend, have no idea of his whereabouts, I'd better inform the police.'

'Yes, I agree,' Harvey said. 'I wish I could help you — not only because you want him but because he is one of my best friends. Only thing I can think of is that he perhaps suddenly got a big idea and decided to walk off and think it out. I've known him do that before today.'

'I don't propose to wait and find out,' Roberts responded. 'I'll call the police immediately. Thanks . . . '

Harvey watched the chief-of-staff stride away actively, then he turned back to the blueprint. He unfolded it and stared at it without seeing a single thing upon it. Instead he saw an implacable face with muscles bulging at the sides of the jaw, and eyes so pale they looked transparent . . .

* * *

Whilst Dr. Blair knew of the late Hammond's bone disease he had not much to say about it. Instead he gave a résumé of all the aches and pains from which the shipper had suffered — until at last Garth rather stiffly excused himself and sought an interview with Sir Wilson Barnett, in his Harley Street chambers.

Here was a different proposition — a tall lean man with silver hair and a mellifluous voice. In a word, the famous osteopath was one of the few really gracious Englishmen left.

'Mr. Hammond?' he repeated, as Garth and Whittaker — their authority having been duly exhibited — sat on the other side of a big polished desk. 'Why yes, gentlemen. Certainly I examined him — and I have read about his tragic and mysterious death.'

'It is my unenviable task to find an answer to that,' Garth sighed. 'And perhaps you might be able to help me ... Naturally it is no longer a case of breach of ethics since we must have every scrap of information in case criminal proceedings follow. Now, Sir Wilson, you know exactly what kind of a man Mr. Hammond was. Do you believe that if he were run over every bone — *every* bone — in his body would be broken in consequence? He once told me that he was like a walking glass ornament.'

'No,' the specialist replied emphatically. 'In common with other laymen in medical matters, you have an exaggerated idea of the late Mr. Hammond's complaint, Inspector. His bones were definitely of abnormal delicacy, due to congenital disease which we call *fragilitas ossiumtarda* — but the *real* danger of his disease lay in his earlier life when he was still maturing and his bones were, more or less in a state of flux. Back then he would possibly have suffered a breakage of every bone by being run over. But not when he became a man ... Upon maturing he took up a more or less normal life, eschewing only the more violent forms of recreation. His bones were strong enough to carry his weight and he was a fairly heavy man — but the brittle state remained, making him susceptible to fracture from the slightest blow. No, Inspector! His was not a severe case of *ossimtarda*, believe me. I've known worse where the patient is bedridden for life.'

'Then tell me — If he were dropped from an aeroplane from a fair height, would he then break every bone in his body? His bones, as I understand it, resemble beads on a string, each bit of bone connected by tissue.'

'Even under those conditions I doubt the breaking of *every* bone,' the specialist responded. 'A body falling from a height becomes unconscious before hitting the ground: certainly it would be so in a man of Mr. Hammond's type. Blood pressure alone would see to that. That being so he would not fall stiffly, with a jerk calculated to snap his bones — but all of a heap, as it were. Slackly. He was fairly fleshy. That in itself would prevent multiple bone breakages.'

The specialist waited as Garth silently pondered. 'I'm sorry,' he said presently, 'if I seem to be tearing up some of your own theories by the roots.'

Garth smiled. 'On the contrary, sir, you are helping me far more than perhaps you realize . . . Let me trouble you again. Would a fairly average blow with an iron bar, like a poker be sufficient to cause a compound fracture of Hammond's skull?'

'Very probably,' the specialist agreed. 'The skullbone is the hardest of all, of course — with the possible exception of the sternum — but in Mr. Hammond's case it would be fairly soft . . . Yes, it is possible that a blow which would only stun or daze an ordinary man would *kill* him.'

A gleam came into Garth's eyes. 'For that piece of information, Sir Wilson, many thanks . . . Now, there is something else.'

Garth motioned to Whittaker and from the briefcase he had brought with him he extracted several X-ray transparencies and the post-mortem report of Dr. Tenworthy.

'I'd like you to tell me what you think of these plates, sir, and the report,' Garth said, handing them over.

Several minutes passed. Interest changed to amazement on Sir Wilson's lean features; then he frowned in perplexity. At length he put down the report and held the X-ray transparencies to the light of the window one after the other,

'Inspector, are you *sure* this man who was found in Worthing *is* Mr. Hammond?' he asked at last.

'As near as it is possible to *be* sure,' Garth assented. 'I knew him well, and there's no doubt in my mind but that it was him who was found. His daughter has also identified him.'

'But this is incredible!' the specialist declared, looking again at the report. 'Did Mr. Hammond have a twin, do you think?

And perhaps the real Mr. Hammond is missing somewhere?'

'I thought of that, doctor, and I asked his daughter. She says there is no twin . . . However, I'm also having Mr. Hammond's known fingerprints checked with those of the corpse. Those at least cannot lie.' Garth gave a slow, grim smile. 'I think I know why you are hunting so desperately for a twin, sir. It is those misplaced internal organs which are worrying you, isn't it?'

'That's just it! The thing is impossible, and I can prove it! I have X-ray plates of Mr. Hammond, which I took when he first came to me for consultation. I clearly remember that there was nothing wrong with his organs even though there was with his bone structure. In fact I'll let you see them — '

Garth raised a hand. 'That would be a waste of time, doctor. I don't understand X-ray plates and entrails I understand even less. But it is possible that later on your X-ray plates and those of Dr. Tenworthy will be needed in evidence, if only to show that the organs of Mr.

Hammond became mysteriously misplaced without surgery having anything to do with it.'

'As Tenworthy says,' the osteopath mused, 'a man with organs like this would have experienced extreme lifelong pain. Yet apparently Mr. Hammond did not . . . If you know the answer to this particular riddle, Inspector, I'd be glad if you'd tell it to me. It interests me profoundly, from the medical standpoint.'

'And it interests me from the investigative standpoint.' Garth stood up. 'When I've learned more I'll give you the facts . . . You've told me all I need to know and I'm much obliged to you.'

Garth led the way down the stairs from the chambers and slipped into his accustomed seat in the police car. Whittaker clambered in and tossed the briefcase on the back seat.

'What happens now, sir?'

'We have three lines of action,' Garth replied, considering. 'One is to pay another call on Harvey Dell — at the N.T.C. since that is where he'll be at this hour, I imagine; the second is to speak to his friend Clifton Brand who runs the dress salon — and see if he has anything unguarded to say for himself; and the third is to call on the L.C.C. and see what they can do for us with a map of underground sewers.'

'Everything,' Whittaker reflected, 'seems to need doing at once.'

Garth pulled out a cheroot. 'No desperate hurry: things'll fit into place by degrees. What did you think of our interview with Sir Wilson?'

'Well, sir, when I heard Sir Wilson saying all that about the X-ray plates, about the impossibility of such a thing happening, I thought back to electronics.'

'So did I,' Garth said, 'And I remembered reading somewhere about supersonic inaudible sounds which are used to test faults in steel, and which, in one case, accidentally killed a goldfish in a house a mile away. In other words the vibrations had reached that far and the goldfish conked out because every bone in its body was smashed to pulp.'

'Excuse me saying it, sir, but you're off the track. Supersonics have nothing — or almost nothing — to do with electronics. And it seems to be electronics that we're worrying about.'

'So I sit corrected because you read more science than I do. Okay — But look, Whitty, isn't there a *simile*? I mean, if inaudible sound vibration can smash up a goldfish's bones, can't electronics do the same thing to a man? Electronics *do* cause vibrations, I'll swear.'

'They do — under specialized circumstances. But what are you trying to prove?'

'My reasoning runs something like this — One: Dell. Two: Electronic engineer. Three: Broken bones. Four: Electronics might break bones. Five: Dell might be responsible . . . Dropping Hammond from an aeroplane didn't break his bones: running over didn't do it. Electronics *might*. And electronics might have somehow transplanted his innards for him.'

'Yes, sir — all hypothetical,' Whittaker commented. 'And it leaves the biggest slice of the problem hanging in mid-air. Sixty miles in ten minutes . . . *How*?'

'We're just coppers and not scientists,'

Garth complained. 'It isn't fair to *expect* us to solve a thing like this! But we have to keep the chain moving in case we come to a connecting link somewhere. Carry on to Regent Street and let's see what Clifton Brand has to say for himself.'

Before too long a time Whittaker was pulling the car up again outside an obviously fashionable shop with delicate gold-leaf scroll across the windows saying — CLIFTON BRAND'S SALON — EXQUISITE MODELS.

Garth peered somewhat dubiously on the three 'exquisite models' draped on wax women in the window. 'Always gives me the creeps going in a woman's store . . . You'd better come with me.'

Whittaker gave a faint grin at Garth's obvious discomfort. 'Pleasure, sir,' he assented.

'Maybe for you: you're younger than I am. I've got past the days for feminine charm . . . Almost.'

Garth entered ahead of Whittaker through the chrome and plate glass swing doors. Immediately both men were in a world of soft carpets and concealed fluorescent lighting. In the pastel-tinted distances blonde, brunette, and red-headed lovelies glided mysteriously on various missions, their gowns sheathed revealingly to their figures. Upon tall and glittering chromium stands were incredible hats, weirdly designed coats, and preposterous dresses ... There did not seem to be a man in sight.

'May I help you, gentlemen?'

A woman two inches taller than himself and as erect as an empress had materialized. She was perhaps thirty-five, but cosmetics were doing their best to put back the clock.

Garth cleared his throat sharply. 'Yes, I think so. I'd like a word with Mr. Brand, if I may.'

'Is it by appointment, sir? Otherwise — '

'I'm Chief Inspector Garth from the C.I.D.' The production of the warrant card banished the woman's last trace of hesitation and with a rather mystified look she motioned through the midst of the gilded distances. Garth and Whittaker wandered through an embarrassing wilderness of mannequins, potential buyers, semi-clad girls and emasculated overdressed men before they reached a polished oak door inscribed, again in fancy scroll — CLIFTON BRAND.

The woman tapped, vanished within, and reappeared in a moment to motion inside. Garth and Whittaker stepped into a huge office, perfectly appointed, all the harsher details softened either by extreme polishing or color angles. In a word the place seemed feminine. Garth sniffed, as though he expected to smell perfume. Then he directed his gaze to the square desk where a man had risen.

'Good morning, gentlemen . . . '

There was not the least suggestion of anything feminine about Clifton Brand. He was unusually tall, at least six feet four, with rather narrow shoulders. His extreme length was accentuated by his striped trousers and the tails of his frockcoat. Though a black stock tie with a diamond stickpin gave him a mature appearance, he was probably no more than thirty-five. His face was somewhat lantern-jawed, with very high cheekbones.

His complexion was swarthy, his black hair gleaming. Intensely dark eyes with sleepy lids gave him a seemingly insolent expression.

'Mr. Brand?' Garth asked, pausing beside the desk.

'Of course . . . ' Brand smiled. He had a quiet south country voice. 'My manageress said something about the C.I.D. Quite disturbing, I'm sure . . . Do sit down, gentlemen.'

Garth did not beat about the bush. 'When did you last see Mr. Harvey Dell, sir?'

The straight-from-the-shoulder technique proved a little disappointing. Brand merely considered his perfectly manicured nails for a moment and then glanced back across the desk.

'Harvey?' He smiled pleasantly. 'Oh, about a week ago. I'm a friend of his, as I notice you've already discovered. Has something happened to him?'

'Not to him — but something has happened to Mr. Benson Hammond, as you probably know from the news and papers.'

'I don't believe all I read and hear, Inspector,' Brand responded. 'I got the impression that the reporter who wrote up about Mr. Hammond's — er — mysterious death and 'transition' was intoxicated, or something.'

Garth's face was expressionless. Whittaker, his right hand hidden by the bulk of the desk, was taking notes.

'Did you know Mr. Hammond, sir?' Garth questioned.

'Not personally. I'd seen his photograph in the papers and heard of his activities — chiefly through Harvey Dell. Harvey was intending to become engaged to Miss Hammond, you know.'

'Is there any reason why he should not still intend to become engaged to her?' the chief inspector asked sharply. Brand was silent for a while and there was a slight tautening about the corners of his mouth. Garth's pale eyes hardened.

'Mr. Brand, a week ago Harvey Dell was fully intending to become engaged to Miss Hammond. The night before last — Monday — certain events made his engagement impracticable, but I cannot see how you could know of that without seeing Mr. Dell himself much later than the week ago which you mentioned just now. You said Dell was 'intending' to become engaged. The reference to past tense carries a certain significance, you must admit?'

Brand sighed. 'You take things too literally, Inspector. I have been in *touch* with Harvey Dell, but I have not seen him personally. That is what I meant to imply by not having seen him. He told me over the phone of his unfortunate experience with Mr. Hammond concerning the engagement to Miss Hammond.'

'I see.' Garth smiled coldly. 'But why would it matter so much to you whether or not Mr. Dell became engaged to Miss Hammond?'

'If you are trying to make an issue out of this,' Brand said coldly, 'you're wasting your time.'

Garth switched tack. 'Have you ever met Miss Hammond, sir?'

'No, though I have seen her photograph, both in the social periodicals and in snapshots in Harvey Dell's possession . . . ' Brand looked at his wristwatch. 'I hope this is leading somewhere definite, inspector. I'm an extremely busy man. Are you actually accusing me of something in connection with Mr. Hammond's mysterious demise?'

'All I am doing is checking up on Mr. Hammond's death, and that involves all those who might be considered his acquaintances — or acquaintances of his acquaintances. You are a friend of Harvey Dell. Harvey Dell knew Mr. Hammond very well . . . You understand?'

'Not altogether, but I suppose it is the prerogative of the police to sound complicated.' The colour deepened in Whittaker's neck, but he didn't raise his eyes from his notebook.

'Have you any connection,' Garth asked grimly, 'with number nine Stanton Street, W.2?'

'I never heard of the place,' Brand answered.

'You are quite sure you were not present there on Monday evening when Mr. Hammond vanished? Between the times of seven-thirty and eight o'clock?'

'Of course I'm sure!' Brand retorted, stung.

'Then where were you?'

'I don't see that I am called upon to answer that, but if you must know, I was at the Bachelors' Club, just round the corner from here. I'm a member, and spend practically every evening there. It's a quiet, restful place where I can relax and think out plans for new designs.'

'What time did you go there on Monday night?'

'About twenty past six. I left here at five, had tea in a café only a few yards from here — the Mecca — and then went on to the club. I was there all evening. I left again about quarter past nine and went home. You can ask the cloakroom attendant — he'll tell you.'

Garth nodded and got to his feet. 'Thanks, Mr. Brand. Sorry to have bothered you — '

Garth jerked his head to Whittaker and they left the office together, again ran the gauntlet of feminine pulchritude, and so reached the outdoors and their car.

'Can't say I liked Brand at all,' Whittaker said, dropping into the seat beside Garth.

'Yes, Whitty, I agree with you. But did you derive anything from the interview?'

'Not much. Seems to me that he's made up his mind not to say anything. No more than I expected. If Dell won't speak, why should Brand? All the same I'd be willing to wager that he might have been the one who sent that phone call which caused Harvey Dell's about-face.'

'I think he *was* the one,' Garth responded. 'He gave himself away on that when referring to the broken engagement ... ' He glanced at his watch. 'Seems to me that lunch is indicated, then we'd better go back to the office and see if anything fresh has come in. All right — get moving. We'll try the Mecca and check up on Brand at the same time, if we can. That's it down the road there, I think.'

8

Lunch over, Garth sat smoking his cheroot and thinking deeply, jotting down notes as points occurred to him. Whittaker had departed to the Bachelors' Club to check on Clifton Brand's alibi. As far as the café alibi itself was concerned it could not be proved. Nobody remembered having seen Clifton Brand on the Monday evening at teatime.

Half an hour later the sergeant returned to the table. 'Alibi seems to check out,' he reported. 'On Monday night Brand went to the club about twenty past six and checked in his hat and coat with the cloak-room attendant He left again about nine-fifteen, just as he said.'

'Where was he in the three hours in between?'

'A steward says that he saw him in the main clubroom reading, early on in the evening — and he saw him again in the same place about quarter to nine, apparently half asleep . . . ' Whittaker paused. 'Of course, there was nothing in the world to stop Brand leaving the club by a back way, or something, minus hat and coat, and returning the same way. There seem to be a lot of old men in that club — even the stewards — and since Brand spends nearly every night there they probably assumed he was in the club all that time, rather than *knew* he was.'

'In short, an alibi with a doubt in it,' Garth mused. 'All right — just as long as it's been checked . . . Let's get back to the Yard.'

As Garth walked with Whittaker through the café foyer he added: 'Know something, Whitty? Brand's clothes — those striped trousers and the frockcoat — would look just like those of a manservant.'

'So they would! You mean that Miss Hammond didn't see a manservant at all but Brand?'

'She referred to an extremely tall man, and how she noticed the emphasis of light on his cheekbones and jaw. That fits

Brand perfectly. Since he apparently wears that monkey-suit all day at his work, he would hardly need to change it . . . But what the devil were they up to? We'll have to find out who rents that house, or who owns it.' Garth settled in the car. 'Anyway, back to the Yard and let's see if any more surprises turn up.'

Back at the office a variety of reports had indeed come in and been placed on the desk. Garth studied the uppermost report.

'Here is one load off our minds! The letter Miss Hammond received was definitely written by Harvey Dell. Okay, our suspicion about him being a liar is correct.'

Garth picked up a memorandum from the dactylography department. He read it aloud:

''Prints taken of the dead hand of B. T. Hammond are none too clear due to death, but the distinctive features are clear enough to be verified in ten identical instances with prints upon the paperknife submitted. There is no doubt that the body is that of B. T. Hammond . . . ''

'Exit twins,' Whittaker sighed.

'We expected that — Now I wonder what the devil all this is about?' Garth broke off, studying another document. 'It's a report from Grimshaw in Worthing. Take a look.'

Whittaker moved forward and read the report over his superior's shoulder:

★ ★ ★

Telephone Communication from: Inspector Grimshaw, Worthing Police. Received: 12-7 p.m. For: Chief Inspector Garth.

Nissen hut duly investigated. The owner is James Mitchell, aged twenty-seven, who is employed at a Government-controlled research farm in Lancing, where he does laboratory work concerning fertilizers, new feeding stuffs, and so forth. When a series of Nissen huts in the area was put up for sale by the Government he bought the one in question. The others were bought by various firms and dismantled for removal.

I questioned Mr. Mitchell and he replied that he uses the hut as a 'ham' radio station. He has a current Post Office license for transmission and reception of radio. I asked Mr. Mitchell to let me see inside his hut and he raised no objections. I found it filled with radio equipment, which only a technician would be able to fully understand.

I next questioned him about the footprint trails and he explained that he was in the hut last night (he uses batteries for lighting), making some adjustments to his apparatus, but he was not actually broadcasting or receiving. He went — as usual — in a small converted truck (his own property) from the Lancing farm. He explained the footprint trails away by saying that he went to his hut, brought out a heavy piece of equipment and carried it to the truck, went back to his hut to lock it up, and then returned to his truck in readiness to drive away. That makes a total of four sets of prints, with one heavy one leading from the hut — which, in the absence of anything else, seems to explain the matter. I asked him what the heavy equipment was and he showed it to me, still in the truck — an object rather like a very heavy switch-panel . . .

Further instructions awaited.

* * *

'He's been pretty thorough, sir — no doubt of that,' Whittaker commented.

'Uh-huh . . . And once again the old theory of electronics raises its head. Radio is connected with electronics: that I do know.'

'Maybe that's just plain coincidence. There is a flock of radio amateurs like this chap Mitchell scattered up and down the country . . . Just the same, it's clear that the inspector doesn't understand the intricacies of radio any more than we do. Why not have some of our radio experts go down there and look the stuff over? No laymen would ever be able to tell the difference between radio and electronic equipment.'

'If I get tangled up any further I'll do just that,' Garth promised. 'As things stand, I haven't any real reason for questioning this chap Mitchell. Grimshaw seems to have taken plenty of liberties as it is. Mitchell has no known connection with Hammond, and motive is one of the main things we must prove. Far as I know Mitchell isn't even a friend or acquaintance of Dell or Brand. For that reason I can't tackle him on the same ground as Brand . . . '

Garth picked up another memorandum absently and considered it. Then he gave a start and his eyes sharpened. 'Take a look at this one!'

Whittaker did so and read:

★   ★   ★

In accordance with instructions that any messages relating to Harvey Dell, Claire Hammond, or the Noonhill Teleradio Combine should be relayed to you — the following is a transcription of a message received from the Noonhill Teleradio Combine at 12-15 p.m. today:

Caller: Professor Gordon Roberts, chief-of-staff of the N.T.C. research department. He reported the mysterious disappearance of Leslie Carson, a scientist from the N.T.C. Carson has not been heard of since leaving his rooms in Agnes Street, W.C.1, at six-thirty last night. Information has been relayed to Divisional Inspector Anderson who is instituting inquiries.

★ ★ ★

'Now what?' Whittaker was startled. 'Carson is one of Dell's friends — in fact the other one whom Miss Hammond mentioned.'

Garth reached for the telephone. 'Hallo? Get me Divisional Inspector Anderson, or the sergeant-in-charge, right away . . . Hurry it up.'

The crisp voice of the divisional inspector came over the wire. 'Divisional Inspector Anderson speaking — '

'This is Garth, Anderson. I understand you've been tipped off about one Leslie Carson?'

'That's right, and I just got in from a fruitless routine inquiry. According to his landlady — he lives at 27 Agnes Street, West Central — he left his rooms at six-thirty last evening, saying he'd return by nine. After that he seems to have vanished into thin air. He may have walked to wherever he went, which would make it that he wouldn't attract any particular notice — such as the attention of a taxi-driver, or something. I've got two good men doing their best to trace his movements, so far without result. I've also questioned his friend and associate at the N.T.C. — Harvey Dell.'

'Huh! I've had dealings with that secretive young man myself. Naturally he didn't tell you anything?'

'Nothing that was much help, anyway. He last saw Carson yesterday evening when he left the N.T.C., and he hasn't seen him since . . . I was fortunate in getting a fairly good studio portrait of Carson from his rooms and I'm having it published — both through the newspapers and the *Police Gazette*.'

'Good,' Garth acknowledged. 'Okay, Anderson, you carry on. I won't cramp your style: I've enough on my plate as it is. The moment Carson is located advise me. It's possible that he has at least part of the answer to this confounded

Hammond puzzle.'

'With which I'll bet you're enjoying yourself,' the divisional inspector commented, with a dry chuckle.

Garth rang off and sat glowering as he lighted a cheroot fiercely. 'Of the three people likely to explain this problem two of them are tight-lipped enough to make an oyster envious, and the third has vanished!' He picked up another report and scowled at it. 'That alibi of Miss Barrow's checks,' he said. 'She did just as she said. Which finishes her part in the business, as far as I'm concerned.'

Garth looked more homicidal than ever as his interior rumbled. 'The inquest will probably be tomorrow,' he went on, 'and we have got to get something to show for it, otherwise there will be trouble — from the Chief and the A.C. in particular. Blast it, we don't even know that this business *is* a crime yet! Or whether the victim was bludgeoned, run over, taken for a ride, or just plain wafted! And the one person with a real motive, the letter-writer, turns out to be a frustrated secretary with a conscience!'

Whittaker hesitated. 'I'd better get these various statements I've collected typed out, sir. They'll have to be signed and — '

'Do your homework later,' Garth interrupted. He got to his feet and went across to get his overcoat. 'You go along to Stanton Street and have those men on duty report back. They're wasting their time there now, I think. When you've done that find out who the house belongs to. Go to the city planning department — go to the best estate agents — go where in Hades you like but find out who owns or rents that property. Then report back here. As for me, I'm going to the L.C.C. to try and find out all there is about the sewers and waterways of London. We'll meet here eventually and compare notes.'

'Okay, sir,' Whittaker agreed promptly. 'You'll want the car?'

'No, I'll walk. Not far. Must do something to get the digestive juices working.'

★　★　★

It was towards six o'clock when a more cheerful Garth returned to his office. He found Whittaker busy typing up the various statements he had committed to his notebook.

'Any luck, sir?' he asked.

'Definitely. We're about to turn into a couple of gondoliers at seven o'clock this evening — going on a tour of the London sewers and underground waterways.'

Whittaker deserted his typing and came over to the desk as Garth dropped into his swivel chair.

'I also found out where that channel under number nine Stanton Street winds up. It runs into the Thames. It's part of an underground freshwater spring and it has been there for donkey's years. Only it was never known to be there until bomb damage in the blitz revealed it . . .

'At that time,' Garth continued, 'number nine, together with the entire block of houses which is now deserted, was used for something hush-hush connected with the War Office. It was War Office engineers who drilled the shaft from the basement to the stream, and they also enlarged the passage where the stream flows. The idea was so that messages could be carried underground when things were too violent on the surface. When the war ended the War Office gave the place up — and the block — which passed to a private landlord. However a few years ago the property was condemned as unsafe because the entire area around might some day subside into the underground waterways ... That accounts for that entire block, except number nine, being untenanted.

'Later though, the situation was reviewed and the condemnation order withdrawn. The block was put back on the market after engineers, had made a further examination, and found that if any subsidence occurred it would not be for years. The block had a reprieve, and was transferred to the open market for sale as a possible block of temporary flats, or each house individually. Walton, Shand and Gainsborough became the agents.'

'Not only for that particular block, sir, but for all Stanton Street,' Whittaker said. 'I found that much out for myself. And I found out who rented the house.'

Garth gave a slow smile. 'Harvey Dell or the now missing Leslie Carson. Am I right?'

'It was Carson,' Whittaker replied. 'He rented it on a year's lease some five months ago, in June. But how did you know?'

'Because that one particular house has unique basement 'get-away' facilities — the shaft into the stream. Since both Dell and possibly Carson have previously worked for the government, they could have seen the records of the back-room scientists during the war, who worked in that very house. I think both of them knew the possibilities of the house and of the two it was Carson who did the renting. Naturally he would be hand-in-glove with Dell. There may even have been other reasons, too, besides the 'get-away' possibilities.'

'But what about Clifton Brand?' Whittaker asked. 'He isn't remotely scientific.'

'I don't know what his connection is, Whitty — at the moment. By the way, have some tea sent in will you? I'm nearly passing out.'

Whittaker nodded and left the office. He returned after giving his order and asked another question.

'Since everything was above board — in that Carson rented the place in his own name and signed a lease — why on earth do you imagine he, and perhaps Dell, wanted a house with the means of a quick get-away?'

'That,' Garth said, 'is purely a matter of assumption. But we *do* know that they were up to something secret — witness the boarded window in the cellar. That automatically implies that somebody else might want to *learn* that secret. That being so, a wise man makes preparations for a quick departure if necessary.'

'Even to the extent of adding dust and giving the impression that nobody had ever *used* the place? That it had been used was more or less evidenced by the light in the front room . . . '

'As to that,' Garth responded. 'I think the dust was an additional elaboration. Whoever was in number nine at the time of the 'vanishing act' had never bargained for what happened — hence the tremendous efforts to try and prove the place had not been used for months — despite the front-room light. That light, I think, was merely to give the impression that people lived normally within, whereas they actually worked very abnormally in the cellar upon something or other.'

'Confoundedly involved,' Whittaker muttered. 'You mean that with the house apparently not having been used for months, it was hoped that it could never be proved what happened to Hammond — or perhaps to Leslie Carson either?'

'That's the way I see it,' Garth responded, glancing up as a constable brought in the tea on a tray. For a time he and Whittaker were silent as they gave their attention to the tea and sandwiches; then Garth said:

'I've made arrangements to explore the underground stream tonight. I gather it's easily wide enough to accommodate a motor-launch. We're meeting two L.C.C. officials at the East Dock, Pier seven, tonight. They'll show us where the stream comes out into the Thames — then we'll go 'upstream' until we come to the shaft.'

'It might be a good idea to dredge the stream under the shaft whilst we're at it,' Whittaker said.

'We will. There will be tackle aboard the launch for small-scale dragging anyway.' Garth got to his feet and took the evening paper from his overcoat, spreading it on the desk. Whittaker looked at a man's photograph.

'So that's Leslie Carson? Looks a pretty brainy type.'

'No fool, I'll gamble that.' Garth sat down again. 'With that in the evening papers let's hope he might be found somewhere.' He became moodily reflective. 'If we don't find some clue either in the shaft or the stream bed, I'll have to hold up my hands and admit myself beaten. 'Case Uncompleted',' he added bitterly. 'And it would be the first time it happened since I became a C.I.'

'There'll be something,' Whittaker said confidently.

'Normally, yes — but in this case we're dealing with scientists and when they get up to their tricks we ordinary blokes are just left floundering.'

'No reason why we should,' Whittaker responded and as Garth gave him a questioning glance he added, 'it's an old adage to set a thief to catch a thief. Maybe we should set a scientist to catch a scientist. I'm thinking of Dr. Carruthers.'

'*That* tea-drinking madman!' Garth exclaimed. 'Things are not as bad as that, surely?'

'Carruthers may be a madman, but he's one of the cleverest scientists I've ever known — And you know it, too, sir. Oh, I know he calls himself the 'Admirable Crichton' of science — but that's just his conceit. Maybe he has a good reason for it, too — There are few to touch him in physics, atomics, and similar sciences. We'd be in a bad way without him. Remember how he sorted out that messy little fire-raising business in Halingford last year? Every bit of the scientific fitting-together was his doing and — '

'Oh, blast the man!' Garth snorted, irritated. 'I'll have to be really down and out before I'll call on him. He's insufferable! Forget the idea — and it's time we were moving,' he finished, with a glance at the clock.

Whittaker and Garth left the office together and got into the car. As usual Whittaker handled the driving, arriving at Pier seven, East Dock, at exactly seven o' clock. In the mist of the winter night, hardly visible in the dim string of pier lights, were two men muffled in over-coats.

Garth exchanged brief greetings with them and then clambered down into the waiting motor-launch, water slapping noisily beneath its bows. Whittaker and the two L.C.C. officials descended after him — then with a roar the motor-launch moved away into the mist.

'The stream you are looking for comes out at a sewage vent,' the senior official explained. 'In fact three sewers and the stream combine, to emerge at one opening in the Thames. It's not very far from here. Once we're inside, it is merely a matter of taking the right channel.'

'Do you suppose,' Garth asked, thinking, 'that any man could swim against the current at the entrance to the sewer?'

'Not a chance — unless he took it at high tide. When that happens the water level rises and reverses the current for a distance of perhaps half a mile. Even then there's still room for a launch to get along. In the ordinary way, at low tide, the sewer opening is some six feet above the level of the water. Tonight we'll be on the flood tide and sail right in.'

Both he and Whittaker fell silent, content to leave it to the man at the wheel to find the way — which he did, through the mist and chilly darkness. The searchlight on the prow of the launch suddenly blazed into being and before the watching men there loomed an enormous circular opening of glazed brick embedded in a gigantic circle of ironwork. Into it flowed the grey water of the river, combined with sewage. As the boat chugged into the tunnel an overpowering odour rose.

'This won't last long,' the senior official

mumbled, from the folds of his handkerchief. 'Once we get into the clear water tunnel we'll be okay.'

The brilliant beam of the searchlight cast on glazed and gleaming walls, lined on each side by raised footpaths fitted with rusted iron rails. The noise of the motor-launch's engine was deafening in the confined space.

For half a mile the huge bore extended, then out of the blackness ahead there loomed four openings. Three of them were obviously ancient. The fourth central one was more recent and hastily contrived. From a distance it looked small, but it grew in dimensions as the launch came closer to it and finally sailed into it, progressing fiercely against a swiftly moving current. Presently Garth lowered his handkerchief and sniffed the air cautiously. The mephitic stench had gone.

'We're all right now,' the senior official said. 'The shaft you're looking for is about two miles farther on. As you'll notice, this bore isn't too well made. It was the best the War Office engineers could do in a short time.'

Garth looked about him. Here there was no glazed brick or raised footpaths — only this fast-flowing torrent of water sweeping out of the distance ahead, and the sides of the tunnel propped up with massive seasoned timbers and, here and there, iron stanchions. The whole arrangement of underpinnings looked horribly unsafe.

Scowling, he stood watching and waiting with Whittaker beside him; then at length the launch began to slow down and at last came to a stop, the water racing past it in a noisy cataract as hooked poles anchored the boat to the rough walls of the tunnel.

'There!' the senior official said, and the searchlight beam was swung so that it directed upwards.

Immediately overhead was a wide expanse of shaft going up into darkness, at the limit of which was the dimly visible iron network of the grating in the basement of number nine Stanton Street.

'The roof of this tunnel is about six feet above us,' Garth said, 'containing the shaft — that hole there. Only way to get at that is with a ladder. Which is the only way *anybody* could do it I imagine.'

'I thought of that,' the senior official said. 'We've a light-weight extension-ladder here which should do the trick . . . ' He turned to one of the crew. 'Get it fixed up, will you?'

In the reflected light of the searchlight beam there was considerable activity for a moment or two as a light metal ladder was run up in sections, climbing up into the shaft with its base supports set squarely on the center of the launch's deck.

'There it is,' the senior official said finally. 'Staircase to heaven, inspector. Don't worry, it'll take all our weight.'

Gingerly at first, Garth and Whittaker began ascending. Slowly they mounted the entire thirty-five-feet distance, then Garth stopped with the massive circular grating of the cellar manhole-cover immediately above him. Down below the searchlight beam glared upwards from the launch's deck.

'One thing's certain, sir,' Whittaker

remarked, standing on the rungs immediately below, 'nobody would be able to do anything in this shaft without either a ladder or a rope . . . '

Garth did not reply. He was working the massive bolt of the manhole-cover back and forth. It moved easily, its slots well greased, a fact to which he drew Whittaker's attention. Satisfied on this point at last, he left the bolt across, looked about him, and suddenly pointed.

'There we have something!' he exclaimed. 'Take a look!'

Whittaker was already doing so. Driven into the wall about six inches below the rim of the manhole-cover socket were two massive staples perhaps a foot apart. Nor were they particularly old. So far rust had not collected on the gun-metal grey coating they both had. They had been driven in at a slightly upwardly tilting angle.

'Evidently somebody put those in by reaching down through the open manhole, sir,' Whittaker said. 'What's your guess about them?'

'I'll make just one — They have been

used to hold a metal ladder of some kind . . . You gather, then, how the dust on the grid in the basement is accounted for?'

'I think so,' Whittaker responded, pondering. 'Whoever it was coated the cellar floor in dust, walked towards the manhole, and then climbed into it. He got on to the ladder and lowered the manhole-cover into place. The next thing he did was poke the nozzle of the dust-blower through the grating's center and work it for a few moments. That caused the grating to become covered in dust. The person then descended a ladder — one similar to this maybe — and so probably reached a boat already moored in the stream below. All he had to do then was lift the ladder from the staples and then . . . Well, we don't know. Maybe the ladder was thrown in the water.'

'Quite a competent reconstruction,' Garth said approvingly. 'Which also tells us that the thing for making dust was hand-operated because there would certainly be no power on tap in this shaft — At least I don't think so. The matter of power supply has me pretty bothered.'

The chief inspector studied his surroundings again and at length gave a nod.

'Okay, we've more or less solved the problem of the cellar. Let's get down below again.'

Slowly he and Whittaker descended the rungs back to the launch's deck.

'Any luck?' the senior official inquired.

'I think so,' Garth responded. 'What I'm anxious to find out now is if there is anything in the bed of this stream. You brought the dredging tackle?'

The official nodded and gave some more instructions. The glare of the searchlight was removed from the shaft and instead was concentrated on the area immediately around the anchored launch, the brilliance glinting on the churning, muddy water as it boiled and rushed past the vessel. Then two of the crew began to get to work over the side with long hooked irons, nets, and objects like harpoons.

'You mightn't think it,' the senior official said, 'but this water is about twenty feet deep. We may not even be able to do anything with the tackle we've got.'

In this he proved to be correct. Though every effort was made and a full hour taken in dredging, the results were negative. All that came up was yellowish mud. At last Garth shook his head.

'We're wasting time with these methods,' he said. 'And from the look of this mud the bed of this stream is extremely soft. Whatever may have been thrown into it has perhaps become buried under the ooze. That leaves only two answers, because I have got to have the bed of this stream explored — Either a diver must be employed, or the stream must be temporarily diverted.'

'The latter method would be best,' responded the senior official. 'A diver wouldn't be able to stand much chance in this fast moving current; at least not enough chance to make a thorough examination such as you want, Inspector. Two miles farther up this bore there is an old disused one from a sewer. We could divert the main body of the stream down there perhaps — at least enough to permit of an examination of the bed below.'

'That's more like it!' Garth exclaimed. 'How long do you think it would take?'

'We could do it overnight with sandbagging and props, and start examining this bed tomorrow morning whilst the dam holds. It won't stand up for long, of course, but long enough for our purpose, I think.'

'Right.' Garth gave a nod. 'Do that, and let me know when something worthwhile turns up . . . For the moment we've all done what we can here — and many thanks for your co-operation.'

9

Garth returned to his office at the Yard with Whittaker. The sergeant's secret hope that it might perhaps be possible to get to a home fireside a bit earlier for once was dashed as the chief inspector squatted in his swivel-chair and lighted a cheroot.

'Let's try once more to fit the pieces into place, my lad,' he said. 'First: the cellar was obviously all prepared for a getaway down the shaft; Second: we can be pretty sure that a boat would be standing by at the base of that shaft, either of the rowing or motor-boat type; Third . . . Blast!' he broke off, as the telephone shrilled.

'Yes, Garth speaking,' the chief inspector responded, to the voice — muffled to Whittaker — at the other end of the wire. 'Oh, it's you, Anderson . . . Yes? Mmmm?' Garth sat up straight. 'What!' he exclaimed. 'Drowned, did you say? You had him taken to the mortuary?' Pause. 'You bet I will! I'll be over right away. Many thanks.'

He slammed down the telephone and got to his feet.

'Leslie Carson's body has been found! Some schoolboys playing about where they shouldn't near the East Side wharves came across it about an hour ago. Seems one of them had seen tonight's paper and recognized the corpse's face. The boy called the police while we were playing about in the sewers and the buck was passed to Anderson who's in charge of that part of the business. Let's be on our way.'

As Whittaker drove the car through the busy London streets he asked a question.

'What do you make of Leslie Carson being drowned, sir?'

'Not much as yet. But since the body has been washed up out of the Thames, and not more than a couple of miles from where that shaft stream comes out, it's likely that Carson was also present in that house in Stanton Street. Maybe he fell down the shaft, or was thrown down

— Maybe lots of things! Can't tell much until we've seen the body and had the doctor's report.'

'At least if Carson was murdered we know we're looking for a murderer,' Whittaker said. 'With Hammond we've never been sure — but this is different.'

'What was the motive for silencing Leslie Carson, I wonder?' Garth muttered. 'Who silenced him? Harvey Dell, or our sleek friend Clifton Brand with his rocky alibi?'

Garth fell silent. Eventually Whittaker stopped the car outside the divisional police headquarters where they were joined by Divisional Inspector Anderson.

'Mortuary's a mile farther, on,' he said, settling in the rear of the car. 'Keep on driving, sergeant; I'll direct you.' Whittaker obeyed and started the car forward again.

'Anything particular to tell me, Anderson?' Garth asked.

'Nothing fresh, I'm afraid. The divisional surgeon should be busy with his examination when we get there. As far as that poor devil Carson himself goes, the only sign of identification is his resemblance to his photograph. His pockets are stripped clean of clues. No wallet, no anything. His shirt and collar have the laundry marks on them, though, so I suppose we could prove through them that he *is* Leslie Carson. I've had his landlady informed and she should be along to make an identification . . . '

'Do you think,' Whittaker asked, keeping his attention on the road, 'that perhaps Carson caused Hammond's mysterious transition and then killed himself?'

'It's a possibility,' Garth sighed. 'I wouldn't like to pass an opinion until I've seen the body.'

Whittaker finished the journey to the mortuary as rapidly as safety allowed. Then with Garth and the divisional inspector he went into the dull, cheerless building and through to a back tiled room where, under a bright light, a smallish man was just at the end of his task.

''Evening,' he acknowledged, in a matter-of-fact voice, glancing up. 'I'm just about ready to go — '

'Any doubt that this chap was drowned?' Garth asked, turning down the sheet and looking at the dead, bloated face.

'None at all,' the divisional surgeon responded. 'But I don't think that drowning was the *cause* of death. I think his immersion in the water finished what had previously been manual strangulation. Signs are unmistakable. The swollen condition of the neck was not produced by water but by hands . . .

'Death by drowning,' the divisional surgeon went on, 'is probably one of the most difficult deaths to assess. The paleness, the temperature, the adipose of the skin, or its maceration — All those things might point either to drowning or, equally, to something else. In this case, the fellow's shoes — as is natural — are so tight that they'll need cutting off before he's put down: that bears out the immersion theory all right. But what I find as definite proof that he was killed first is that whilst his stomach contains river water, and a good deal of it, his lungs do not. A drowning man, alive, draws water into his lungs as well as air. In this case that did not happen.'

The divisional surgeon closed his bag decisively. 'Strangulation — and the body thrown in the water afterwards which prevented all chance of recovery if life was not entirely extinct. He died about twenty-four hours ago. Best I can do for you. I'll send in my full report to headquarters.'

'Thanks,' Anderson responded absently. 'Good night, Doctor.'

The doctor left the cold, inimical room. Then Whittaker spoke. 'That makes it murder.'

'Uh-huh.' Garth glanced up. 'If it does nothing else it narrows the field. Carson didn't commit suicide, anyway, so that leaves only Harvey Dell or Clifton Brand for it as the main culprits — unless Hammond was responsible, which I doubt. Of the two men likely to have the strength to commit manual strangulation there is nothing to choose between Dell and Brand.'

'Then you have two suspects in mind?' the divisional inspector asked.

'Yes.' Garth gave him a glance of apology. 'Sorry, Anderson, I was forgetting that you don't know our end of the business.' He recounted matters as far as they had progressed.

'Nasty, sticky mess if ever there was one,' Anderson commented. 'I suppose you're taking on this part of the job now?'

'I shall have to, since it's all part and parcel of the same thing. Not that there is anything to take on,' Garth shrugged. 'Leslie Carson is dead, and that's the end of it. The reason why he's dead is a complete mystery — '

Garth paused and glanced up as a police constable came in, a small, elderly woman at his side. She gave a timid glance about her and stood waiting, playing with her gloves.

'Mrs. Chedworth, I expect, Carson's landlady,' Anderson murmured. 'I sent for her to make an identification . . . ' He walked forward.

'So sorry, madam, to have to inflict this on you, but it has to be done, I'm afraid. You happen to be the nearest available person capable of identifying the body. All we wish to know is: is this Leslie Carson?'

Anderson took the woman's arm gently and she advanced. As unostentatiously as possible he raised the sheet and the woman looked steadily — then she jerked her eyes away and bit her lip. Slowly she nodded.

'Yes . . . Yes, that's young Mr. Carson,' she assented. 'But whatever happened to the poor boy, Inspector? He didn't seem to me to ever have an enemy in the world — and he certainly was never depressed.'

'For your edification, madam,' Garth commented, 'Mr. Carson was not a suicide — as you seem to believe. He was murdered.'

'Murdered! But who on earth — ?'

'I wish we knew,' Garth said grimly. 'Normally we don't pass on the information that a man has been murdered, but in this case time is very important to the police. So you might as well know the truth. Whilst you're here I'd like to ask you a question or two.'

'Yes. Yes, Inspector, of course.'

'A chair for the lady, sergeant,' Garth ordered, and waited until his instruction had been obeyed. Then as the woman sat down rather shakily he continued. 'Mrs. Chedworth, did Mr. Carson ever speak of a Mr. Dell or a Mr. Brand in your hearing? Or perhaps of Harvey or Cliff, referring to Christian names?'

'Not as far as I can remember,' the woman answered finally. 'No, I'm sure he didn't. In fact, the only person he ever referred to with any regularity was a friend by the name of Jimmy Mitchell.'

Garth gave a start. 'Did you say Mitchell?' he asked sharply. 'Are you *sure*?'

'Oh, yes. I particularly remembered it because it happens to be the name of my brother as well. I was a Miss Mitchell before I married.'

'Mmmm . . . Jimmy Mitchell.' Garth thought swiftly. 'About how long ago did Mr. Carson refer to him?'

'I can't exactly remember — but certainly quite a time ago. He used to refer to him quite a lot — and I think he spent some of his weekends with him last summer. He lives down in Lancing somewhere, I believe. Anyway, towards mid-summer Mr. Carson — or Leslie, as I used to call him — stopped making his trips and ceased referring to Jimmy Mitchell. Why, I didn't know, and it was not my business to ask.'

There was visible exultant glow in Garth's pale eyes.

'Is there anything else you can tell me?' he asked. 'No matter how irrelevant it may seem to you.'

Apparently there was not. Mrs. Chedworth seemed to have completely run out of information. Garth nodded as she rose.

'Thanks very much, Mrs. Chedworth. See the lady safely home,' he added to the constable, and watched her leave with the policeman's tall form behind her.

'That hut in Lancing!' Whittaker exclaimed, when he, Garth, and the divisional inspector were together again.

'Exactly!' Garth was beaming, his jaw muscles bulging. 'That was one turn-up I didn't expect. I'd almost forgotten that chap Mitchell with so many other things on my mind.' He became pensive. 'So he ceased visiting Mitchell towards mid-summer, did he? Mmmm . . . Whitty, when was that lease taken out on 9 Stanton Street?'

'June this year, sir. I forget the exact date but I've got it written down.'

'June's enough. Now let's hazard a guess. About that time something of a secret nature came into being, and this chap Jimmy Mitchell was somehow linked up with it. Perhaps for that reason it became necessary that he be the odd man out, so to speak — seeming to have no connection with the other three in the London area. So, visits to him by Leslie Carson, his friend, ceased — and Carson also ceased speaking of him, perhaps in the hope that his connection with him would be forgotten. What it all proves,' the chief inspector finished, sighing, 'I'll be thrice damned if I know! But to find out that Mitchell is part of the set-up and that he was nearest the body of Hammond when found — or at any rate his radio hut was — is news indeed! That chap is due for an interview!'

'And in the meantime?' Anderson asked.

'There's nothing much can be done

as far as you are concerned,' Garth responded. 'There'll be an inquest on this chap, of course, and it'll be adjourned — same as the inquest on Hammond, which is due tomorrow. Since this chap had no relatives that's the end of it. Advise the N.T.C. that he has been found drowned, believed murdered. If you don't tell 'em the newspapers and media will do it anyway . . . As for me I'm going back to my lair to do some thinking for tomorrow. Come on, Whitty.'

10

Garth's intention to go 'back to his lair' proved, to Whittaker's satisfaction, to mean going home — except for a brief call at the office on the way.

The following morning they both met at the office again at nine o'clock and, despite a good deal of thought, neither of them seemed to have crystallized any particular conclusion.

'No news from those engineers busy on the underground stream yet sir,' Whittaker said.

'Maybe it's all to the good.' Garth reflected. 'I shan't feel so unhappy about having to take time out to go to the inquest at Worthing.'

'Whilst you're there, sir, do you think it would be a good idea to have a word with that chap Mitchell?'

'No, I don't think there would be much to be derived from it at this stage. Grimshaw has already questioned him and we have the facts — as far as Mitchell is prepared to give them at this stage . . . I think I'll tackle him when I feel I've got something really worthwhile with which to pinpoint him. Now we'd better be on our way.'

It was three o'clock in the afternoon before they returned with the inquest adjourned pending the completion of official inquiry. 'Well, sir, we didn't squeeze much more juice out of that,' Whittaker commented. 'Dell still sticks to his story. Miss Hammond told everything she told us — '

'Didn't expect anything else, did you?' Garth asked, going over to his desk. 'That's why I deliberately played down my hand. I don't want anybody to know how far I've got in case the guilty one moves faster than I and removes something important somewhere in the way of a clue — Good!' Garth broke off, studying a report on his desk. 'That stream bed is all clear and men are working on it now.'

He reached for the telephone and in a moment or two was talking to the senior official of the L.C.C. who had the job in hand.

'There's no particular reason why you should waste your time on the spot, Inspector,' the official said, in response to Garth's inquiry. 'Especially now the stream is temporarily dammed up it means having to wade through slime and filth. We'll find whatever there is — if anything — and fetch it to you.'

'Okay,' Garth responded. 'And many thanks.'

He rang off and sat thinking. Whittaker did not need to ask questions. He had overheard the conversation. But he did ask a question of another kind.

'I've been wondering, sir . . . Do you think Harvey Dell is such a well-paid scientist that he can really afford a place like he's got? It's no pig-in-a-poke. Hardly the place you'd expect to find a Government scientist. They're not usually millionaires.'

'Harvey Dell may have private resources,' Garth replied, 'of which we know nothing — and which, as yet, we have no authority to inquire into; or, being a scientist, and most probably an inventor on the side, he may do well out of royalties.'

'Not that well, sir, or he wouldn't have needed to badger Hammond for two million quid.'

Garth mused. 'I see what you mean. A man in obviously comfortable circumstances, and yet anxious to borrow more? You've got something on your mind, my lad. Let's have it!'

'All right, sir. I suggest that in the ordinary way Harvey Dell would be living in pretty much the same circumstances as the late Leslie Carson lived; or maybe in slightly better surroundings since he is in seniority to Carson. The fact that he lives in a swank apartment house I attribute to outside money. And I think his social position was arranged so that he could become engaged to Miss Hammond, herself having a wealthy background, without difficulty. Once that was done, as it very nearly was, it looks to me as though the idea was to get two million in a hurry.'

'So you think Dell's attempted engagement to Miss Hammond was for business, not love?'

Whittaker nodded. 'If anybody is financing Dell I can only think of Clifton Brand, with his prosperous-looking gown business. Carson had no real money, and this chap Mitchell doesn't seem to have either. So finance may have been provided by Brand, who could be the master-brain in this whole complicated business.'

'Yes,' Garth admitted, 'it's an interesting speculation, and I think we'd better verify it. Any information we can get at all which proves a connection between Harvey Dell and Clifton Brand is useful, and if we can rope in any contact with Jimmy Mitchell as well, so much the better.' He glanced at the clock. 'Miss Hammond ought to be home by now. She said she was returning from Worthing by the next train. She has the funeral details to attend to for tomorrow.'

'We could ring her up and be sure,' Whittaker said.

'We could — but if she's not in the mood for visits she might stall us, and I don't want that. We'll just drop in.'

Whittaker, who had not yet taken off his topcoat, re-buttoned it. Garth thought to himself and switched on the desk-phone.

'Garth here,' he said, as a voice responded. 'Tell a photographer to get a good full face and full length of a chap named Clifton Brand. He runs a dress salon in Regent Street and it ought to be possible to get a glimpse of him going in and out of the place at some time. Don't let him know what you're up to. Use a plain van, infra-red plates if it's dark — Anything you like, but get me those photos.'

'Right, sir,' the voice responded.

Garth switched off and caught Whittaker's questioning eye. 'When I've got those photos, I'm going to have one of them touched up by the photography department and then let Miss Hammond see it. She may thus be able to identify the servant she saw ... Now let's see what she has to say for herself.'

Both men left the office together and went down to their car. The transition to Maida Vale was soon accomplished under

Whittaker's expert driving; then Hilton was standing in the poor light of the November afternoon, gazing out from the front doorway.

'Miss Hammond at home?' Garth inquired, and his eyes strayed to a glow of light from the windows of the lounge.

'If you'll step inside, gentlemen,' Hilton invited, holding the door open wider.

Garth and Whittaker did so, hats in hand.

'This way, gentlemen, if you please.'

Garth entered the lounge, Whittaker following. Then he paused momentarily. He had not expected Harvey Dell to be present as well.

'Miss Hammond — Mr. Dell.' Garth looked from one to the other of them and nodded. 'I'm sorry to disturb you, but this is a matter of some urgency.'

'Of course, Inspector,' the girl said quietly. 'Please sit down. You too, Sergeant.'

She moved silently in her black dress and switched on the main lights. They seemed to harden the already set face of Harvey Dell as he stood beside an easy chair, defiance in the tautness of his mouth. He was in the same clothes he had been wearing at the inquest.

'I think I'll be going, Claire,' he said. 'Since — '

'I'd rather you stayed, Mr. Dell,' Garth interrupted, a smile transforming his death-mask expression. 'What I have to say concerns you as much as Miss Hammond.'

As Claire gave him a meaning nod and seated herself, Harvey shrugged and followed suit on an easy chair.

'Mr. Dell came back with me on the train from Worthing,' the girl explained. 'Chance led us to have the same compartment and we patched up our differences. We are engaged again.'

'My congratulations,' Garth said, his light eyes fixing on Dell's stubborn face and then shifting to Claire again.

Claire gave a troubled little smile. 'Har — Mr. Dell will be attending the funeral tomorrow morning — '

'It was not chance which led Miss Hammond and I to be in the same compartment, inspector,' Harvey put in.

'I knew that with a fifty-mile train trip ahead of us Miss Hammond could not possibly walk out on me — and it gave me the chance to explain a lot of things.'

'I see. You wouldn't like to explain them to me, would you?'

'One would hardly explain to a police inspector as one would to one's fiancée,' Harvey snapped.

'I agree, Mr. Dell — but there must be some matters equally of interest to both of us. I believe the main cause of your breaking off the engagement was the letter you sent, which started Miss Hammond on a wild-goose chase to Stanton Street. Is that mystifying little episode now cleared up?'

'I'm satisfied Mr. Dell did not write it. It must have been a joke on somebody's part,' Claire said quickly.

Garth smiled faintly. 'Miss Hammond you love Mr. Dell quite a lot, don't you? You are willing to ignore the real facts just as long as you can become engaged to him?'

'Now look here, Inspector!' Harvey demanded. 'It's no concern of yours if we become engaged, is it?'

'None at all,' Garth admitted slowly. 'What is my concern is the strange death of Mr. Hammond, to say nothing of his transition to Worthing. I have to include in my inquiry all peculiar, unresolved happenings, and in particular that letter to Miss Hammond. You did send it, Mr. Dell! Our calligraphists have proved it!'

Harvey remained silent and the girl glanced at him sharply.

'However, I had another reason for coming here,' Garth continued, watching Harvey intently. 'I'd like to know when you first met each other.'

'Why?' Harvey inquired sourly.

'Nothing wrong in a question like that, is there?' Claire asked him in surprise. 'It was in June. Inspector. We met in a box at the theatre. The place was crowded and Harvey had to share the box with Dad and me. From that things . . . just grew.'

Garth nodded. 'Just about the same time, in fact, that the late Leslie Carson rented 9 Stanton Street.'

'Did you say — the *late* Leslie Carson?' Harvey Dell asked sharply.

'I did. Haven't you read the papers?'

Harvey shook his head. 'I was too busy thinking about getting to Worthing to bother with a newspaper. How about you Claire?'

'I merely glanced but I didn't notice anything,' she replied. 'What does this mean, Mr. Garth?'

'Since you haven't been to the N.T.C. today you don't know the facts, of course,' Garth said, still looking at Harvey. 'Carson was murdered two nights ago and his body was thrown in the Thames — the same night on which Mr. Hammond's strange behavior occurred . . . If you're thinking of denying all knowledge of Carson's existence, Mr. Dell, I shouldn't. Miss Hammond told me he was a friend and workmate of yours, and the N.T.C. knows it as well.'

'I'm not denying anything,' Harvey answered, a look of profound worry crossing his face. 'Of course he was my friend — my best friend, in fact. Murdered! My God, I never thought of that . . .'

'Never thought of it?' Garth repeated.

'How do you mean?'

'I mean that I knew he had disappeared, of course, and that the police were being told. Professor Roberts of my department told me about it. But for Les to have been murdered — It's horrible!'

The chief inspector did not say anything for a moment. Claire seemed a little paler and a good deal more agitated. Harvey stared straight in front of him as though he still could not believe what he had heard; then a thought seemed to strike him.

'Look here, Inspector, what did you mean by Leslie renting 9 Stanton Street when Miss Hammond and I first met? What has that got to do with it?'

'It is possible, Mr. Dell, that it may have a great deal to do with it. So far, though, you have not co-operated with me one little bit. That being so why on earth should I tell you what kind of conclusions I've reached?'

Claire turned and reached out her hand to grip Harvey's arm.

'Harvey, if there is any way of clearing

up this dreadful business, for heaven's sake speak!' she insisted. 'You've done nothing wrong. I'm sure of it! So what have you to be afraid of?'

'If you don't speak, Mr. Dell, you'll be the loser in the end,' Garth said.

Harvey remained silent, his brow crinkled with moody thought.

'All right,' Garth said, a glint in his eyes. 'Since you won't tell me anything I'll tell you how things look to me: then maybe you'll see the danger you're in by keeping silent ... I suggest that your social position, particularly exemplified by that fine flat you have, was deliberately created last June as a background for your association and ripening friendship with Miss Hammond. In your ordinary capacity as a Government scientist you could never have arrived at equal terms with Miss Hammond and her millionaire father — so to get over that difficulty an apparently moneyed background was created.'

Garth raised a hand as both Claire and Harvey stared at him.

'Don't get excited,' he warned.

'Though the whole thing, I'm convinced, started out as a business proposition — even to the meeting in the box being arranged to make a start — I don't deny that you both perhaps fell genuinely in love with each other into the bargain. No reason why you shouldn't — but I do believe it all began as a business deal. What is more, I have a pretty good idea who financed the idea.'

Garth glanced at Harvey. 'It wouldn't be policy for me to mention names,' he said. 'But you know perfectly well, Mr. Dell.'

'I'm afraid I don't,' Harvey answered stubbornly. 'And your theory of a business deal is about the craziest thing I ever heard of!'

'I don't think it is — not when I remember that you asked for a loan of two million pounds the moment you felt sure that your engagement to Miss Hammond had her father's blessing.'

Harvey gave a start and glared at the girl.

'I — I overheard some of the things you said, Harvey, that's all,' she explained. 'So of course I told the inspector, since he wanted to know everything.'

'I'll further suggest,' Garth continued, 'that you were connected with something highly secretive which had its lodgment in 9 Stanton Street. I'd say that you had something which needed money to develop it — so ways and means were found for you to become engaged to one of the wealthiest young women in town, with the main idea of getting her father to help financially. Things went wrong and Mr. Hammond wouldn't have anything to do with it.

'Three things, Mr. Dell, stand out before me. First, you met Miss Hammond in June when your social background was established; second, Leslie Carson rented an old house, possibly for secret research, also in June; and third Leslie Carson, who was a great friend of a young man named James Mitchell, who lives in Lancing, ceased all visits and communication with that young man in June. Those three points add up to something, and if you don't tell me what I'll be obliged to put whatever construction I can upon them, detrimental to you or otherwise.'

'I'm afraid you've linked up a lot of coincidences,' Harvey said, shrugging. 'I wouldn't be fool enough to add anything to help you believe them.'

'I also have the hope, Mr. Dell, that you will not be fool enough to obstruct justice,' Garth commented. 'It's only a question of time before the rest of the story comes out. Why can't you be frank with me?'

'I've even less reason now,' Harvey retorted. 'I've been pretty sure all along that you've suspected me of being connected with Mr. Hammond's death — which I wasn't — and now my friend Leslie Carson has been murdered you probably think I did that too! Only an idiot would start telling tales at this time. You do what you like, Inspector. I prefer to keep quiet and see what happens next.'

'If you think Mr. Dell had anything to do with my father's mysterious death, Mr. Garth, you're utterly wrong!' Claire declared. 'He couldn't. He just *couldn't*.

Do you think I would ever have patched up our differences and decided to become engaged to him if I entertained the slightest doubt?'

'I have not said,' Garth responded, 'that I consider you guilty of anything yet. Mr. Dell: that's purely your own idea. I'm giving you the chance to clear the air. If you don't then you can't blame me for what may happen in the future.'

Harvey hesitated and the girl seized his arm again.

'Harvey, it can't do any good any more to deny that you sent that note to me. Since experts have proved you wrote it, you must have done. Why *did* you send it?'

Harvey looked at her steadily. 'I still say it was somebody's joke. As for experts — Well, even experts make mistakes.'

'Do you also deny,' Garth asked, 'that you were driving your own car when Miss Hammond saw you pass by?'

'Emphatically! As I've already convinced Miss Hammond, she must have made a mistake in the registration number. It only approximated mine, and she mentally adjusted it to appear to be the same.'

Garth got to his feet, his face hard and unsmiling. 'I'm sorry you've taken up this stand, Mr. Dell. Now I think I'll be on my way. Ready, Sergeant?'

Whittaker nodded. Neither the girl nor Harvey made any move to accompany the two men from the room. They were shown out by Hilton, and returned to their car in the growing dimness of the November twilight.

'Dell's a pretty obstinate bloke,' Whittaker commented.

'He's a fool to himself,' Garth retorted. 'I'm as good as sure in my own mind that he isn't responsible for either the death of Hammond or Carson, but he's so scared of being involved that he won't play straight. Just the same, I think he got a shock at hearing of Carson's murder. I have the impression that up to that point he didn't know that Carson was even in danger.'

'Do you think,' Whittaker said pensively, 'that perhaps Dell has been thinking all this time that Carson caused the mysterious death and transition of Hammond, and that he — Carson — then disappeared? Now Carson has been murdered Dell knows differently — namely, that somebody else might have been at the back of the Hammond business. Maybe Clifton Brand. Or even that chap Mitchell.'

'That's a pretty good theory,' Garth admitted. 'The chances are that up to now Dell has not known the real facts about Hammond — that he was probably murdered by a blow on the head, the weapon having disappeared, and then transferred to Worthing. If he thought Carson did that he perhaps assumed it was an accident, or something, and that if Carson could get away with it he — Dell — was not going to say anything to involve himself . . . But now Carson's murdered it is a different story. He knows the heat will be turned on. He may even have the sense to think things over and walk in the office to explain himself. Perhaps he didn't want to before Miss Hammond.'

Whittaker switched on the ignition. 'At

least we've proved more or less conclusively that his moneyed background was a deliberate set-up for catching Miss Hammond, and that it was contrived at the same time as number nine was rented . . . The Yard, sir?'

'Yes. I'm anxious to see if anything has turned up from that stream bed — And it also occurs to me that I'll have both Dell and Brand kept under observation from now on, and keep tabs on their respective telephone wires — private and business. It is just possible that now he knows of Carson's death Dell may make a move to contact Brand and get some facts from him.'

Whittaker drove swiftly through the traffic in the gathering dusk and brought the car back to Whitehall and Scotland Yard some thirty minutes later.

'I'll be damned!' Garth exclaimed, as he entered the office and switched on the light.

'After all, sir, you asked for it,' Whittaker grinned.

Garth advanced slowly. On a sheet of tarpaulin on the floor there had been laid an extraordinary assortment of stuff, most of it cleaned of mud but bearing obvious traces of having been in water. Garth turned as a constable came in.

'Oh, you're back, sir. I just heard — '

Garth turned pale eyes on him. 'This lot is from the L.C.C., I suppose?'

'Yes, sir — came whilst you were out. The L.C.C. official wants you to ring him up. I was on duty and told them to — '

'All right.' Garth jerked his head briefly. 'Thanks.' The constable departed.

Garth did not immediately inspect the stuff: instead he stuck to business and instead instructed two men through the interphone to keep a watch on Harvey Dell and Clifton Brand. This off his mind he returned to the assortment and went down on his knees to study it. Whittaker joined him.

There were objects that were obviously radio components, though the glass had been smashed from them and the filaments and grids had been crushed. There were also objects like voltmeters small drums wound with wire, which, despite water immersion, still retained the warm glint of bare copper. There was also a big semi-circular object like a magnet, with what appeared to be electrodes jutting out of each end. These were the major exhibits. Other oddments comprised sheets of ebonite, perspex, and wafer-thin metal blades such as might be found in a condenser.

'Interesting,' Garth commented, sitting back on his heels. 'At a rough guess a radio set has been smashed to blazes . . . I'd better ring up the L.C.C. and find out what I can.'

He went to the desk, gave his telephone instructions. Soon he was speaking to the senior official. 'Thanks for the Christmas box,' Garth said. 'Even if I am no wiser than I was to start with.'

'That's all the smaller stuff, inspector,' the official said. 'There's a pile more. Couldn't put it in your office so I had it brought here. You can come and view it any time.'

Garth snatched his cheroot from his teeth. 'A pile more?' he repeated in surprise. 'Such as?'

'We first found an extension ladder,

each section of which slides into the other. It's fifty feet when fully extended; ten when not — but not too heavy for one man to carry. Then there is something resembling a flywheel — a big, perfectly made thing, which looks as though it has been unbolted from a spindle. There's also a hefty-looking device, which looks like some kind of generator with a lot of fins on one end . . . Those are the main things. There are also a lot of steel bars with screw holes in them — rather like the sides of an old-fashioned bedstead — plates of metal, aluminium legs with joints, bracing bars . . . Oh, a pile of stuff! Nothing's left in that stream bed now. We dredged it clean.'

Garth was slowly recovering from his astonishment and looking at the notes he had made on the notepad. 'All right, thanks very much. I'll be over to have a look at the stuff the moment I can.'

11

Whittaker, who had partly overheard the voice in the receiver, looked at the notepad as Garth pushed it towards him. He glanced up under his eyes.

'Go on, say it!' Garth growled. 'I'm no nearer! The only thing in the whole issue that makes sense is the extension ladder.'

Whittaker said thoughtfully: 'I can understand that whoever made the getaway would not take any heavy stuff for fear of overloading the launch, or whatever it was — but a few things like these presumed radio equipment parts, and panels on the floor there wouldn't have worried him. Neither would the extension ladder. Why did he leave those behind to be found? It completely gives away the secret of the basement, how it was escaped from.'

'It may have been a much safer bet for him not to have been seen with an extension ladder and mysterious equipment in his boat,' Garth responded, thinking. 'He may even have met somebody whom he didn't wish to see the stuff. Besides, there was at that time no safer hiding-place than the mud of the stream bed. It is we who have been smart in digging the stuff out.'

'I suppose so, sir. And now we've done it what do we do? I can't get beyond thinking that it's radio equipment.'

'Neither can I — but we'll go further than that. What's our scientific department for, anyway?' Garth snapped on the desk-phone, which connected with the special scientific department attached to forensic. Its job was mainly research, taking over when forensic ingenuity came to an end, and keeping track of all the latest devices employed by up-to-date criminals.

'That you, Harry?' Garth asked, and, as Superintendent Harry Bates assured him that it was, Garth added: 'Step along to my office for a moment, will you? I've some lovely stuff for you to look at.'

'Easy as that,' Garth said, switching off.

'Mmm, five o'clock. Order some tea, Whitty, will you?'

Whittaker nodded and left the office. He had barely departed before a man in a white overall came in, holding a sheaf of prints between finger and thumb.

'Photographs for you, sir,' he said. 'Clifton Brand.'

'Eh?' Garth gave a start. 'Oh yes! Who took 'em? You?'

'No — Foster. I just developed them. Pretty good. You can have as many prints as you want. If there's anything give me a buzz.'

Garth studied the six prints carefully. Two were first-class full-face views of Clifton Brand, one with his hat on and looking supremely satisfied with himself; the other with his hat off and him looking extremely annoyed. There were two pin-sharp full-length shots of him in Regent Street, attired in his frockcoat and striped trousers. The two remaining photographs were blurred and spoiled.

Whittaker returned from giving tea instructions and came over to the desk as Garth motioned him. 'Yes — nice work,' he agreed. 'Except for those two duds. Looks like some of Foster's work?'

'It is,' Garth responded, and snapped on the desk-phone. 'Get me Foster in the photographic department,' he instructed, and in a moment Foster came on the line.

'Hallo, chief! Those what you wanted?'

'Couldn't be better — and the one of him without his hat is just what I wanted.'

'The first time, where he has his hat on, he was leaving the store in mid-afternoon. When he came back, about ten minutes later, I had Charlie go out of the van, mingle with the streetwalkers, and collide with Brand. In the process he knocked Brand's hat off. Notice his annoyed expression? Anything else?'

'Yes. I want you to doctor up that particular shot so that it looks as though a light is shining down on the face from above. You know — emphasize the points that would he visible if the night was dark and there was only a single lamp overhead. Then do the same for the full-length figure. Think you can do that?'

'With the equipment I have here I'll do it in no time,' Foster chuckled. 'I'll set to work on the job right away. You can keep those prints.'

He switched off and Garth nodded to himself in satisfaction — then he glanced up as Superintendent Harry Bates came in, looking more like a well-seasoned sportsman in his golfing trousers and alpaca jacket than the head of the scientific department.

'All yours,' Garth said, waving a hand to the stuff lying on the tarpaulin. 'And when you've got through with that there is another load of stuff over at the L.C.C. offices — equally peculiar.'

Bates frowned and rubbed his jaw as he stared at the assortment, then with a shrug he flung the four corners of the tarpaulin over the equipment and heaved it up on to his shoulder.

'Tell you later,' he said. 'I'll have to get some of the boys to help me with this — '

'Don't make it *too much* later,' Garth warned. 'Whatever you discover about that lot might be the first real clue I've had in a confoundedly baffling business.'

Bates nodded but he did not commit himself. Whittaker held the door open for him to leave, and left it open as the tea was brought in.

Garth stubbed out his cheroot in the ashtray and reached for a cup of tea. 'We started on this business with nothing but an empty house laden in dust. Since then were found out — One: How the dust was probably laid; Two: How the 'dust-layer' escaped; Three: That some sort of radio equipment was in the cellar and later ditched down the shaft; Four: That Harvey Dell, Clifton Brand, the late Leslie Carson, and one James Mitchell all have a connection with one another, Five: That Harvey Dell became acquainted with Claire Hammond for the sole purpose of finance to commence with, and then later apparently fell really in love with her; Six: That there is money, but not enough of it, in the background; Seven: That Brand is probably the source of that money since he is the only likely one; and Eight: That Harvey Dell, if he did not commit murder, is probably trying to conceal somebody who did.'

'Apart from the report on that stuff

that Bates has got what is the next move?' Whittaker asked, as he munched a sandwich.

'To prove that there is a definite contact between Dell and Brand. After that,' Garth tapped his finger on the desk, 'it will become possible to break Dell down and make him tell the truth if only to save his own skin. And there is Mitchell to deal with, too. He'll keep for the moment, though.'

Whittaker took another sandwich. 'And when we've had tea we'll go along and see Miss Hammond with those touched-up photographs, I suppose?'

'You will,' Garth responded. 'I've no time: I'm waiting to see what Bates has to say about that stuff he's got. From Miss Hammond I want you to find out if, to her, the photographs look like the manservant she saw. If so — Okay, then our guess is right. Brand was that servant.'

'Suits me,' Whittaker assented. 'Miss Hammond's a nice girl — '

'And you're a police-officer supposed to keep his mind on his job!'

Foster had the retouched photographs ready in half an hour. Garth studied them and nodded, handing them over to Whittaker. He left the office at quarter past six. When he returned towards seven he found his superior sitting morosely in his swivel chair, a half-burned cheroot jutting from his lips, a blank, grim look on his emaciated face.

Garth seemed to be in the grip of one of his fiercest dyspeptic attacks. 'There's an inquest on Carson at eleven tomorrow,' he said morosely. 'I just heard.'

'Oh . . . ' Whittaker wondered if this had caused the gloom.

'How did you get on?' Garth growled.

'Splendidly! Miss Hammond hardly hesitated when she looked at the photographs. She is certain that that is the man she saw.'

'I expected that. And since she has never seen Brand personally she's had no chance to notice the connection — a fact of which he is aware, of course. All right, so the manservant *was* Brand.'

Silence. Whittaker waited, wondering if he had committed some grievous sin.

'Oh, hell fire and blast!' Garth exploded suddenly, banging his fist down on the desk. 'Whether I like it or not, I've got to go and have a word with that tea-drinking madman, Dr. Carruthers! I'd ask him to come here only I know he'd refuse. Conceited little upstart!'

Whittaker gave a faint smile of relief at discovering that he wasn't under a cloud.

'Our own scientific department hasn't the remotest idea about all that stuff in the tarpaulin and at the L.C.C.!' Garth went on. 'Even the great Bates is in the dark, and I certainly am. He sums up with the bright observation that the stuff might belong to radio equipment, and equally it might not! He says that the components are unlike anything he ever saw and of no known make. The coils and windings are foreign to him. As for that horseshoe-shaped thing, he says it is part of a big magnet, the purpose of which he can't even guess at. That being so,' Garth finished, 'I'm either to admit myself beaten here, or see if I can get Carruthers

221

to do something.'

Whittaker nodded. 'And if he can't, sir, we're stuck.'

'I've been talking to both the Chief and the A.C.,' Garth added. 'They agree that Carruthers should be consulted — and since they are above me that's that . . . I'd better ring up and see if he's at home. What's his confounded number?'

Garth stood scowling as Whittaker calmly picked up the telephone. 'Halingford, seven eight,' he said, and waited. First a woman's voice replied — then a man's, high pitched and impatient.

'Yes? What do you want?'

'Dr. Carruthers?' Whittaker inquired gravely.

'Whom else did you expect? What *is* it? I'm busy — '

Garth took the phone, removed his cheroot, and spoke with very unconvincing good humor.

'Hallo there, Doctor! This is Garth speaking — C.I.D.'

'Garth? Garth?' repeated the irate voice. 'Oh — Chief Inspector Garth, you mean? Well, well! What kind of a mess are you in this time? That's what you must be in or you wouldn't ring me up. You're not in love with me, you don't send me a card at Christmas — so you wouldn't bother ringing now only you want help. Huh! You boys at the Yard make me tired.'

Garth cleared his throat and looked homicidal. 'All I want, Doctor, is an interview with you — and it is extremely important. I can come over now if you'll see me.'

'See you? Of course I will! It'll be an excuse to have some fresh tea brewed — Come when you like: middle of the night for all I care. I don't waste my time sleeping like you chaps.'

The line went dead with an emphatic bang.

'Insufferable!' Garth whispered. 'And I don't see anything to grin at!' he flared at Whittaker. 'Look up when there's a train to Halingford.'

Whittaker picked up the timetable and scanned it, hunting for details concerning the small southern town some thirty miles from London where the volcanic Dr. Carruthers resided. 'There is a train in ten minutes, sir. I can just get us to the station in time.'

'Just as long as you get me, that'll do,' Garth responded, bundling himself into his topcoat. 'You'd better come back to the office and get those statements finished — and stay on hand in case those boys watching Dell and Brand send in any news. I should be back by ten.'

Whittaker whirled him to the station at top speed. During the journey Garth sat in a corner seat of a crowded compartment and brooded on the misfortune that had driven him to seek aid of the self-styled 'Admirable Crichton' of science.

His mood was still black as he sat in the taxi that bore him from Halingford station through the main street of the town and finally into quiet suburbia where lay Sundale Avenue and the home of Dr. Carruthers.

Halfway up the avenue Garth alighted, paid the driver, and began walking slowly. He knew the house he wanted for he had been there before. It was the only house of its kind in the road — Georgian, with two round pillars at either side of the portico — and surrounded by a low iron rail, which separated the gardens from the road.

Garth opened the iron front gate and walked up the long pathway. He stopped in the portico and pressed the bell. After a moment a light appeared in the hall. The door opened and a dour, middle-aged woman became visible.

'Good evening, Mrs. Barret,' Garth greeted.

'Oh, it's Inspector Garth! The doctor's expecting you. I'll — '

'It's all right,' Garth interrupted, removing his hat. 'I know where his study is. I'll go right in.' Garth strode down the long hall to a door at the extreme end, facing the front door. He tapped

'Don't stand knocking,' a voice called out.

Garth cleared his throat and entered the room beyond. He noticed that it was in no wise changed from his last visit. There was a massive desk with bulbous legs, its top utterly buried under mountains of papers, charts, and several blueprints. Against the walls were filing cabinets, a massive safe, and three bookcases of varying sizes, their shelves crammed with books. The only other furniture consisted of a dented and well-used easy-chair drawn to one side of the imitation marble mantelpiece, and several small bentwoods in various directions. A bright fire crackled. The entire panorama of confusion was lighted by a brilliant high-wattage lamp depending from the ceiling in a golden-yellow shade.

Garth's gaze shifted to the man at the desk. He was scribbling as though his life depended on it. All that was visible was a massive head with gray hair sprouting from it in a Beethovian-like mane, rather narrow shoulders, and small hands. Dr. Hiram J. Carruthers, PH.D., D.SC., ex-boffin and backroom boy, was wearing an old jacket with frayed cuffs and streaks of ink on one sleeve where he had slashed his recalcitrant fountain-pen from time to time.

''Evening, Doctor,' Garth said, stopping at the desk.

'Sit down,' Carruthers ordered. 'Find a

chair. There's one somewhere . . . I'm busy.'

Garth found a chair and sat down to wait. At length Carruthers finished his task and tossed down the pen. He looked up and there was revealed a curved nose and jutting lips and chin. Sky-blue eyes, faintly humorous and definitely cynical, surveyed Garth insolently. 'You're a bit fatter,' Dr. Carruthers said.

'I didn't come here to discuss myself,' Garth snorted. 'I'm here because I've got to be. The Yard needs you.'

'But I don't need the Yard,' Carruthers responded. 'In fact, I regard the police as an infernal nuisance — Have a cigarette. One somewhere.'

Carruthers's hand slapped violently on the mountains of papers until he struck something hard. He drew a lacquered box into view with an air of triumph, and opened it. Garth nodded his thanks and then jumped as a queer-fangled lighter flamed in front of his eyes in the eccentric physicist's skinny hand.

'Can we get down to business now?' Garth asked.

Carruthers got to his feet, drawing hard at his own cigarette. He was unusually small, no more than four feet ten, with the body of a schoolboy — in un-matching trousers and jacket with a tobacco-ash-dusted waistcoat — and the head of an Einstein.

'Depends what you want,' he said. 'I'm hard at work on diatoms — a new monograph for which my publisher is waiting. Gordon, my secretary — Mr. Drew to you — is in London with his wife getting some scientific information for me.'

Garth shifted position. 'Quite so. My business concerns Benson T. Hammond, the shipper who — ' Garth stopped. Carruthers was grinning impudently, revealing very white false teeth.

'The moment I read about Hammond, I knew you boys at the C.I.D. would scratch all your hair out trying to get to the bottom of it. He moved from south London to Worthing in ten minutes, didn't he? And it's been played down in the newspapers because it's so outland-ish. Interesting. Very interesting.'

'More like exasperating,' Garth stated, dragging hard at his cigarette in an effort to get from it the same kick as a cheroot. 'I've got most of the investigative side in fairly good shape, but I admit that problem of Hammond's transition has got me beaten. Even our scientific department has fallen down on the job as well . . . So the Assistant Commissioner suggested I should ask you to help.'

'Have some tea?' Carruthers invited, and with an unerring dive of his hand into the papers he pulled out an aluminium teapot with a knitted cosy round it. He opened the lid and peered inside. 'Nearly cold,' he sighed. 'I'll have Mrs. Barret fix us up.'

He pressed a bell-push somewhere under the desk edge and pressed it. There was no response. 'Maybe she didn't hear,' Garth said.

'My housekeeper heard all right. Two buzzes mean fresh tea: it's a standing order. An extra buzz at an interval of precisely four seconds means add one cup and saucer for a visitor . . . '

'To get back to the Hammond

business . . . ' Garth began.

'I have of course formed several conclusions as to what happened to Hammond,' Carruthers said insolently. 'The best thing you can do is give me the facts from start to finish — Here, sit in the armchair. Mind the spring in the middle.'

Garth transferred himself to the armchair by the fire and loosened his overcoat. Carruthers whirled up one of the bentwoods and settled on it.

Overawed by the little scientist's compelling personality, Garth went through the entire story, holding nothing back. The tea arrived when he was halfway. He had drunk one cup to Carruthers's three by the time the tale had been told. The physicist sat staring into the fire.

'Interesting,' he mused, his eyes narrowing. 'Naturally, the detection part doesn't concern me in the least: I've no time for peeping and prying. Give me a scientific problem and the police can take care of the rest . . . As to this particular business I think you're up against a genius in this Harvey Dell character. I knew him slightly when we both worked for the Government. Though I didn't tell him so I admired his ability, particularly in the field of radar and radio television. That chap's before his time.'

'It'll be a pity, then, if I have to arrest him in the finish for murder. Cut his career short.'

'Murder be damned,' Carruthers said politely. 'Dell's incapable of even swatting a fly. The thinkers rarely are: that's left to the brutish ones. Dell may be keeping quiet from a mistaken sense of loyalty, or some valuable secret which would be betrayed to outside inimical influences if he said too much.'

Garth took a cheroot from his case absently and lighted it. 'I like Dell myself, in spite of everything. Since you seem pretty sure of him, too, that narrows our field to the villain of the piece being either Clifton Brand or James Mitchell . . . Anyway, that's *my* problem. What are you going to do about this body-moving business?'

'Look into it — because if it is what I think it is, it's something without precedent in either scientific or criminal history. Just the same, I don't quite understand why your scientific department couldn't get to the root of it. Only conclusion I can arrive at is that they haven't all the parts in the puzzle.'

'The L.C.C. said they'd dragged that stream absolutely clean.'

'Then there remains the possibility that some parts, exclusive to this mysterious junk yard which has been dug up, may have been taken away . . . '

Carruthers stood up. 'I'll be over at the Yard first thing tomorrow to see what I can do. Can't make it before then: I've got this chapter of my book to finish first. Once you get your mind geared to higher physics, you can't let go until you're finished. Since your problem has waited this long a few more hours won't hurt it.'

Garth rose and buttoned up his overcoat. 'Okay, Doctor. I'll expect you tomorrow morning — and thanks.'

Carruthers grinned. 'Don't thank me, Garth: I'm always glad to find something unusual — and to show you masterminds at the C.I.D. how far you fall short of public expectation.'

Garth left the confused, untidy room. Evidently that mysterious bell-push had been operated again for Mrs. Barret appeared magically to see him out at the front door.

Broodingly, Garth went down the long pathway and began the short walk to Halingford station.

12

Towards eleven Garth arrived back at his office. He found Whittaker seated taking it easy, his reports completed. 'Seen him, sir?' he inquired.

'I have — and he's as insufferable as ever. However, the upshot is that he'll be here tomorrow to see what he can do. If he did nothing else he cleared my mind a lot concerning Harvey Dell.' Garth related what had happened and Whittaker mused over it.

'What we'll have to prove then, is why Dell is keeping quiet and who actually killed and transferred Benson T. and murdered Leslie Carson.'

'That isn't going to be easy, Whitty. Meanwhile, any news from those boys watching Brand and Dell?'

'Oh yes! Report came in about half an hour ago. They have neither of them made any attempt to communicate with each other, either personally or by phone.'

Garth scowled. 'That makes it seem that they won't because finding out about Leslie Garson's murder was fairly urgent from Dell's point of view. He's damned wary! Perhaps he has guessed we'll have him taped.'

'Once we've unraveled the scientific implications behind all this you can probably force his hand, sir,' Whittaker said.

Garth glanced at the desk. 'Those statements ready for signing?'

'Yes — all of 'em.'

'Okay — get them fixed up tomorrow some time, before the Carson inquest if you can . . . For now, that's all. It's time we saw what the inside of our homes look like for a change. Come on.'

Whittaker did not need telling twice and followed his superior from the office. They walked together as far as the corner of Whitehall and there parted — until nine the following morning.

Garth arrived some minutes later than Whittaker and upon entering his office gave a start of surprise at beholding a gnome-like man with the head of a

Beethoven pacing the office slowly. He was wearing an expensive but overlong fawn overcoat with a massive collar and a twisted belt. On the edge of the desk, upside down, was a black Homburg.

'Hallo there, Doctor!' Garth exclaimed, closing the door and turning to shake hands. 'Didn't expect you so soon.'

'I said this morning, didn't I?' Carruthers gave a glare. 'You should be at work by seven, same as I am. You Yard fellows are always sleeping! Cha! No time for it!'

Garth gave Whittaker a grim look and then returned his attention to Carruthers. 'I'll show you where the stuff is, Doctor, if you'll come this way.'

The little physicist followed the chief inspector through the grey, cheerless corridors and finally into the annex which comprised the scientific-research department. Superintendent Harry Bates was just getting into his alpaca jacket.

Garth returned his salutation and added: 'This is Dr. Carruthers. You may have heard of him — '

'May!' Carruthers bristled. 'Any scientist who is worth his salt *must* have done!'

'Yes, Doctor, I've heard of you,' Bates acknowledged, smiling and shaking hands. 'The chap who takes on where others leave off, eh?'

'Let the doctor see everything from the underground stream,' Garth instructed. 'And when you've finished, Doctor,' he added, 'I'll be in my office until about quarter to eleven — then I've Carson's inquest to attend.' He left the department hastily and returned to his office.

'Shall I get on my way with these statements, sir?' Whittaker inquired. 'I want signatures from Miss Hammond, Harvey Dell, Clifton Brand, and Miss Barrow, granting she's still working at the same place. If not, I'll find her.'

'Whip round as many of them as you can,' Garth responded, 'and join me at the coroner's court for Carson's inquest. It will be adjourned, of course, same as Hammond's was.'

After Whittaker had departed Garth lighted a cheroot, drew a sheet of paper to him, and began writing down the relevant points in the case. He only made notes at all to pass the time pending the return of Carruthers.

Nine-thirty became ten-thirty — Carruthers came into the office without knocking, his black Homburg pushed on the back of his grey mane. He wandered slowly to the other side of the desk. Garth waited, expressionless.

'Yes, a genius!' Carruthers declared finally, glancing up. 'Now I've seen that equipment, or what there is of it, I'm sure of it.'

'I'm only interested in the cause of Hammond's mysterious transition,' Garth said. 'What *is* that stuff I had dug out of the stream?'

Carruthers grinned and sat down. 'I haven't the slightest idea. Looking at the stuff, and I agree with Bates that I'm no nearer now than when I started. All I can identify are revolutionary types of radio components, coils wound in a way I never heard of before, and the introduction of a powerful magnet, the purpose of which I can't fathom.'

'Bit of a comedown for the 'Admirable Crichton' of scientists isn't it?'

'Comedown!' Carruthers echoed. 'Dammit,

man, what else do you expect when you've only half the stuff? I'm a scientist, not a magician — I wouldn't even attempt to pass an opinion on that stuff without having all of it. Get me every part, then I'll show you something.'

'To the best of my knowledge every part is there.'

'That isn't good enough. Parts of vital importance have been removed. I think some small transformers of unusual design are possibly missing, together with inductance coils with special windings, which fact would govern the magnetic field . . . They wouldn't be particularly big — but without them the remains of the apparatus don't make sense.'

'You do think it has something to do with radio, then?' Garth questioned.

'No doubt of it . . . ' Carruthers got to his feet. 'I've told the Superintendent to have all that stuff sent along to my laboratory at home. I'm going back with it in the van: I don't want anything to get lost. In my own laboratory I've got apparatus for testing, and a teapot handy for stimulant. I'll do what I can with what

I've got, but don't expect any miracles without the entire equipment.'

'I'll have the L.C.C. dredge again,' Garth decided. 'I've got to know the answer to that stuff.'

'You do your part, I'll do mine,' the diminutive scientist answered, shrugging. 'And by the way, there's something that might interest you. You told me last night that that house in Stanton Street had lights of a sort without tapping the ordinary power mains. What do you imagine provided light?'

'Batteries. Probably in series.'

'Wrong!' Carruthers grinned and his dentures gleamed. 'You also said that the house was used because it had a convenient bolt-hole in that shaft. Well, that was probably right — but it's only half the answer. Hasn't the other half dawned on you?'

Garth remained silent, tight-lipped.

'Power for the lighting, and maybe for this fantastic and puzzling equipment as well, was obtained from a highly modern type of turbo-generator. That was it — that object with the fins sticking out on one end of the shaft. The other end would normally be balanced by the flywheel, which had been taken off. For your information, a turbo-generator is driven by water power — sometimes by steam-jet power. The blades are rotated. The faster the water's current the greater the revs of the generator and the higher the power produced. That generator has most of its parts in the general debris and my estimation of it is that it originally weighed about eighteen hundredweights and would develop a horse-power of around two thousand from that fast-moving stream.'

'And *that* produced the lights and power for — whatever it was?' Garth questioned.

'Natural to think so, isn't it? Which explains the other half of the reason for that basement being needed. The generator was originally on a massively made stand, the remains of which are to be seen in those separate bars like the sides of a bed — and the queer, jointed legs. My guess is that the generator was unbolted from its stand and then pushed into the stream where it fell in the mud, after which the stand was taken apart and the parts submerged.'

'And would you need two thousand horse-power for dim lighting?'

'I should think not!' Carruthers retorted. 'All that power was for that mysterious equipment, I imagine — But that turbo-generator is a lovely job,' he broke off, wagging his head. 'Not too heavy: in fact, portable, for all practical purposes. I never saw one quite like it. No engineer's name on the cowling or parts, unfortunately. Looks as though a private designer built it and had the parts made, which he fitted together for himself.'

'Harvey Dell, I'll bet!' Garth muttered. 'And it also suggests to me that it must have been essential to keep things secret, otherwise the ordinary power lines would have been used, wouldn't they?'

'Probably,' Carruthers agreed, musing. 'But there would have been a terrific load on them at times. Might have been complaints from the power house engineers.'

'Which would have meant inquiry,

maybe information in the paper in which the address of 9 Stanton Street would have been given away — Yes, it's not very difficult to see why a private turbo-generator was used, and also why a fast-moving stream had to be under the basement. Thanks for clearing that up.'

Carruthers turned as the door opened. One of the men from the scientific department came in. 'We're ready to go now, sir,' he said, glancing at Carruthers. 'Van's loaded up.'

The physicist nodded and put his hat on the back of his head. 'Get the rest of that stuff!' he told Garth, and with a nod of complete finality went out of the office.

'Easier said than done,' Garth muttered, and picked up the telephone. 'Get me the L.C.C.,' he ordered. In a moment or two he was speaking to the senior official who had helped him earlier.

'Sorry to bother you again,' Garth apologized, 'but it is highly probable that there are still a lot of parts in the mud of that underground stream — particularly a transformer, or transformers, and inductance coils.'

'There is nothing more there, sir,' the official insisted. 'I supervised the dredging myself and the bed was scraped clean. So much so I told the engineers to set the water flowing again rather than patch up the makeshift dam. The stream's back to normal. Take it from me: there was nothing more.'

'Okay,' Garth responded. 'You ought to know. Thanks.'

'Which can only mean the parts were taken away,' he muttered, putting the telephone down 'To make it impossible for the heavier pieces to make sense if they were found.'

He departed for the inquest on Carson and thought matters out in between times during the hearing. The moment the coroner had adjourned matters Garth left the courtroom and returned to the Yard with Whittaker. His problem was still unsolved.

'Something the matter, sir?' Whittaker asked finally, putting down the reports, which he had succeeded in getting signed before attending the inquest.

'Plenty!' Garth snapped. 'There are

certain vital parts missing from that equipment we found, and Carruthers needs them to make sense of the business.' In detail Garth gave the particulars. 'Now there is nothing more in that stream bed, which suggests the pieces have been taken away by whoever was responsible, and perhaps destroyed.'

'There might be some sign of traces in Harvey Dell's flat,' Whittaker said. 'He may have some prints or designs, or even receipted bills for his stuff which would give us a clue. All we've got to do is try to find them.'

'How?' Garth looked grim. 'We can't take out a search warrant to examine his flat because, for one thing, I can't tell the J. P. what I'm looking for — and for another Dell is not a man who has ever had a conviction, upon the strength of which most warrants stand, nor is he a receiver of stolen property. At present he is a perfectly free citizen even if he is under suspicion, and I've no justifiable reason for taking out a warrant to search. A search warrant, don't forget, only gives authority to a special officer to enter a specific house to search for and seize specified property. We can't even search Brand's place for a possible clue because he's in the same safe position as Dell.'

There was silence. Garth went to the locker and poured himself out a brandy and soda. When he had finished it he gave a slow, grim smile.

'There's only one thing I can do, and I'm going to do it,' he said. 'I can take out a warrant to search under the Explosive Substances Act, by which I shall have the power to search Dell's flat for any machine, instrument, or thing connected with the making of explosive — '

'But there wasn't an explosion!' Whittaker exclaimed

'How do we know there wasn't? All Hammond's bones were broken, and his skull got a compound fracture. Don't you understand, man, that there is no Act in being whereby I can get the necessary authority to search Dell's property — and Dell no doubt knows it which is why he's keeping quiet. So all I can do is use the Explosives Act. In Section twenty-eight, I think it is, there is permission to take out a search warrant on the grounds that explosive substance was used with intent to burn, maim, injure or do grievous bodily harm to Benson T. Hammond. On those grounds I can also search Brand's place if need be, he being an accessory. Once I'm in Dell's flat I'll use my own judgment. I'm in the ticklish position of having to use a subsidiary law to tackle a happening that has no precedent. And I'll risk it,' Garth decided. 'I'll go now and see the J. P.'

★　★　★

Towards mid-afternoon Garth entered the apartment building in which Harvey Dell had his flat, and took the self-service lift to the third floor. His persistent ringing of Dell's doorbell brought no response.

'You wanting Mr. Dell, sir?'

Garth glanced round. A janitor in overalls was coming along the thickly carpeted corridor. 'That's right. Know when he'll be in?'

'He said around six — which is his

usual time. He lets me know in case of visitors. I see him most mornings when he leaves for the N.T.C. Not that he went there this morning: he told me he wouldn't be there until late afternoon because he's attending the funeral of a Mr. Hammond. You may 'ave heard about his queer death, sir.'

'Oh yes, I've heard,' Garth agreed dryly. 'I'm Chief Inspector Garth of the C.I.D. And since you are here what about opening up this flat? Here is my warrant card, and here is the authority to search. You've duplicate keys, I suppose?'

The janitor shrugged, and then pulled a bunch of keys from his overall pocket. In another moment he had the door of the flat swinging open.

'Thanks,' Garth acknowledged. 'And you needn't wait.'

He entered the lounge and closed the door, switching on the light. His gaze passed from the armchairs, chesterfield, and television and cocktail cabinets to a walnut bureau. He went over to it and considered the closed front. Gently he pulled at the knob, but as he had expected it was locked. To open it with a skeleton key was only a moment's work. The lock was not of a very complicated design.

Garth stared at the untidy assortment — memos, letters, envelopes, and odds and ends all thrown together in confusion. Sitting down, he began a methodical examination of everything. Ten minutes later he had come to an end of his task — which had included a search of the bureau drawers — but there was nothing significant anywhere.

He got up, closed and relocked the bureau, then began a slow ambling of the room, gazing at the walls. Behind three of the pictures there was only the plastering, but at the back of a hinged bronze facemask there was what he sought — a wall safe. He opened the circular wooden door and stood looking at the neat but invulnerable combination-lock on the steel operculum. He reflected for a while and then went to the telephone and dialed a Whitehall number.

'Whitty?' he asked presently. 'Get Underfield from the forensic department to come over here right away. He's a lock expert and I've a job for him. I'm at Harvey Dell's flat. Hurry it up.'

For the remainder of the time until Underfield arrived Garth wandered about the flat, looking at everything and touching nothing — then he admitted the small, ferret-faced locksmith as he rang at the flat door.

'You may be able to open the thing,' Garth said, nodding to the safe. 'If you can't, I'll have to get a representative from the makers, and that'd be an infernal nuisance.'

Underfield looked at the knob and calibrated numbers, then he smiled. With delicate fingers he set to work, cocking his ear to the faint, nearly inaudible sounds going on behind the steel plating. Twice he failed, but the third time he succeeded and swung the operculum open to reveal what was really a large-sized pigeonhole sunk into a steel bed beyond.

'Much obliged,' Garth said, and with a nod Underfield departed. Garth glanced at his watch, noted it was four-thirty and that, all things being normal, he had plenty of time before Harvey Dell should return.

Digging his hand into the safe, he pulled out the contents wholesale and carried them across to the table. Most of it comprised documents of no interest to him. It was a rolled-up sheet of drawing-paper with an elastic band round it that finally anchored his attention — and held it. Opening the sheet out flat, he studied a design executed in Indian ink. It was, to his layman's eye, intricate beyond belief. Carefully he flattened it out, switched on the bright desk light so that its glow flooded the drawing. Then he took a small micro-camera from his pocket and raised it to his eye. The shutter clicked.

There was nothing else of significance in the way of drawings, but there were two or three receipted bills, all of them from different engineering firms in Sheffield. Each bill related to steel equipment. Garth photographed all three and again continued his search, but there was nothing more — Except for a bank passbook and two unused chequebooks.

Thoughtfully he studied the passbook, jotting down the items credited and debited for a year back. He did not attempt to reason out there and then what they meant: that he intended to do in the privacy of his office. This brought him to the end of his search. He returned the various documents and papers to the safe, closed the door and respun the combination-knob, and pushed the wooden door and facemask in position again. Then he took the service lift to the ground floor.

Fifteen minutes later he was back in his office at the Yard and Whittaker gave him an expectant look as he carefully removed the micro-camera from his inside pocket.

'Here, take this to Foster — nobody else — and tell him I want the film developed and large-sized prints made. As quickly as possible.'

'Right sir.' Whittaker took the camera and hurried out. When he returned Garth was sitting in his swivel chair, a cheroot smoldering and the notch deep between his eyebrows as he studied the notebook in front of him.

'This, my lad, is interesting. I made copies of certain entries in Harvey Dell's bank passbook. There are four items, amounting to several thousand pounds, all of which have been paid to Sheffield engineering firms. The items themselves have receipted bills, which are on that film you just took to be developed. There is also the interesting fact that two payments of fifty thousand pounds have been made into Harvey Dell's account by Clifton Brand.'

Whittaker nodded. 'Which confirms our theory that Brand is financing Dell. Fifty thousand was probably to pay off those bills, and another fifty for various things — maybe flat expenses, and so on.'

'Precisely.' Garth beamed in satisfaction. 'We now know that Dell and Brand are probably working hand in glove, and that Dell himself is not really moneyed but appears to be because of backing by Brand. Also we proved that Dell is connected with the equipment we found and that, apparently Brand found the money for it. When I'm ready I'll confront Brand or Dell with this information and see what reaction I get . . . I also found two unused chequebooks. Pity about that: had they been used and the counterfoils made out I could probably have been even surer. Presumably there is a third chequebook, which Dell carries with him . . . '

'Yes, sir.' Whittaker looked somewhat troubled. 'And what about that equipment? Did you find any clue?'

'You bet I did — and I photographed it. I think I managed to get the complete design, but only Carruthers can tell us that. Now go and order some tea, will you? I've done enough for one afternoon.'

13

Garth and Whittaker had just finished their tea when Foster sent in the finished enlargements of the photographs Garth had taken. He studied them intently, whilst Whittaker peered over his shoulder.

'That has to be a design of a radio set,' Whittaker declared. 'But it's the weirdest one I ever saw! Yes, and it's also a design of that that junk we dug up!' he went one excitedly. 'Look at that horseshoe magnet — We found that very thing!'

'Uh-huh,' Garth acknowledged. 'Carruthers will enjoy himself no end with this — Ah! Take a look at these receipted bills! All for scientific equipment. It doesn't account for all the money by a long shot, but it's a help. Better let Carruthers see these as well: he may have some ideas about them. Okay, Whitty, you're due for a journey to Halingford. I'm not trusting anybody else with this information. Off you go.'

Whittaker took the prints, put them in the briefcase, and departed. Five minutes later Garth was sipping a further cup of tea, when a constable appeared.

'A Mr. Dell would like to see you, sir,' he announced.

'Okay. Show him in.' Garth lifted the tray full of crockery from the desk to the top of a filing cabinet and then turned as Harvey Dell came in. His good-looking face was angry.

'Good evening, Mr. Dell,' Garth greeted him blandly, motioning to a chair.

Harvey Dell ignored his proffered hand and sat down. 'Inspector,' he snapped. 'I want to know what the devil you mean by snooping around my flat.'

'How did you find out?'

'The janitor told me. After that I went through my flat, and found that you had been playing around with the bureau and the safe. How you got into the safe beats me. And in any case what *right* had you to do it?'

'I had every right,' Garth responded, settling at the desk. 'I only did it because you have persistently kept your mouth shut. And as to my authority . . . ' Garth withdrew the search warrant from his breast pocket and tossed it forward.

Harvey Dell read it and then gave a start. 'You used the *Explosives* Act as an excuse? Why, it's illegal! I'll have my solicitor — '

'I don't think so,' Garth interposed quietly, returning his wallet to his pocket. 'The death of Mr. Hammond, in which you are involved, might have been caused by explosives which smashed every bone in his body. The fact remains that I have searched your flat legally. I'd never have done it had you helped me when I asked you. I did warn you at the time.'

Dell looked deflated.

'Very shortly, Mr. Dell, there is going to be a good deal of dirty linen washed in public in regard to yourself. How much of it you can prevent depends on how willing you are to co-operate. I'm asking you again — What is your connection with 9 Stanton Street? It's financed by Clifton Brand, isn't it?"

Dell hesitated, then: 'Yes . . . that's right.'

'And just to keep his name out of it, and yours, Leslie Carson became the renter?'

'Right again. You see, I didn't want my name in it because my job was to socially contact Miss Hammond, and renting a queer house in Stanton Street might have seemed peculiar: and Brand didn't want his name in it because he did not want it known that his finances were at the back of it.'

'And you took that particular house over because you — or Carson — knew of its possibilities from government work there, did you not?'

Harvey Dell stared. 'Who told you that?'

'It's my job to find things out. Right or wrong?'

'Right. It was Carson who knew of its possibilities. He worked in that very house for the government, on scientific hush-hush stuff.'

'And you took it over because it had a stream for electrical power — a turbo-generator — and also a quick get-out to the Thames in case of emergency?'

Harvey gave a faint smile. 'Do I really need to sit here admitting these facts when you seem to have found out about them already?'

'I'm only theorizing, Mr. Dell. We don't know yet who caused the death of Mr. Hammond, or who killed Leslie Carson . . . Do you?'

Harvey remained silent and Garth shrugged. 'Let's go on to something else, then. You did send that note to Miss Hammond, didn't you? Why be so damned obstinate about it?'

'I didn't see how it was possible for you to prove that I *did* send it. Now I find you have calligraphists on the job and have invented a reason for searching my flat I might as well admit the truth.'

'You are sure you are not keeping quiet in an effort to shield somebody?'

'Quite sure!' Harvey answered sharply — too sharply.

'Okay . . . And why did you send that note? What was the purpose of it if you meant to deny it afterwards?'

'I didn't mean to — ' Harvey checked himself.

'No, you didn't mean to,' Garth agreed dryly. 'It was a call on the phone which changed your outlook, *wasn't it?*' He banged his fist down startlingly on the desk.

'You seem to have found out the facts about my effort to create a fake social background, so I could meet Claire Hammond on her own terms,' Harvey answered deliberately, and his eyes appeared quite frank as he looked across the desk. 'I admit that to be so. At the time it started as a business proposition and I fell in love with her in the course of it. The whole thing started as an attempt to get some money — or rather a lot of it. Two million pounds, as you already know. That money was wanted for an invention of mine.'

'Go on,' Garth invited.

'There was only one person who seemed likely — the father of the woman I was intending to marry, and whom I still intend to marry,.'

'Leave out the romance, Mr. Dell, and come to the point. If that money was needed for an invention, why could only

Benson T. Hammond provide it? There are plenty of far-seeing speculators who might finance a worthwhile invention — '

Harvey smiled. 'I agree, providing they have the imagination to grasp its purpose. My invention is so unusual that I knew I could never get a backing for it through the ordinary channels. It could only come from somebody very close to me, who, by the very fact of my being a relative, would be more or less compelled to listen. Hence the scheme to become engaged to Claire first and then tackle my prospective father-in-law second . . .

'Unfortunately I acted too soon in endeavouring to interest him in my invention. He jumped to the conclusion that I was a fortune hunter — which in a sense I suppose I was to begin with, until I really fell in love with Claire. Yet I can't be really called a fortune hunter because this invention will be of enormous service to the community and, once launched, the royalties on it could make me, Cliff Brand, and Les Carson — had he lived — millionaires.'

'Just why did you plunge into the

monetary side of the engagement so quickly?' Garth demanded. 'Surely you guessed what the reaction of a tough business man like Hammond would be?'

'Brand was pushing me to get results,' Harvey responded. 'Though he's been my friend since boyhood he's also pretty ruthless in some things. He loaned money to me to build up the social background, build a model of my invention, and rent that house in Stanton Street — where the model was built — on the strict understanding that he would get his money back tenfold once I had Hammond in tow. It was Brand's pushing demands for quick results that made me overplay my hand and that blew the scheme sky-high. I tackled Benson T. as gently as I could, but it was no use.'

'In short, Brand has a cold, financial outlook — whilst you are un-businesslike and impulsive? That it?'

'I suppose so,' Harvey admitted gloomily. 'I've never made any money worth while even though I've invented plenty of things. Somebody else has always managed to steal the gravy.'

'This particular invention must be *some* invention to need a financial backing of two million,' Garth commented. 'And I believe you chose Benson T. Hammond for another reason — because he happened to be a shipper and interested in matters demanding the carrying of material, such as freight, from place to place. You told him you could cut out all that. Remember, Miss Hammond overheard parts of your conversation.'

'Yes. Mr. Hammond being a shipper had a good deal to do with him being selected as the possible backer,' Harvey agreed, but did not elaborate further.

'And that note?'

'I'd told Miss Hammond that I would write to her. When I got to my flat I thought things over and decided she ought to know the *real* reason why her father had turned down the engagement. I didn't know she had overheard part of the conversation, therefore it seemed to me that she must perhaps be thinking that her father had said 'No!' without any real reason. In short, I made up my mind to show her my invention and so try and win her father back into favour . . . '

'And this invention was in the base-ment of the Stanton Street house — hence the request for her to come alone, destroy the letter you had sent her, and so on?'

'Yes. For one thing I didn't want her father following after her to start bawling me out all over again, and for another I didn't want that note to perhaps drift into the wrong hands in case it might tip off any enemies as to the location of my invention. Claire, I knew, would do as I had asked — only she was not as thorough as I would have liked in destroying that note.'

'Then?' Garth questioned, brooding.

'At the N.T.C. I told Les Carson that I was going to demonstrate the invention to Claire, as a last hope of getting Hammond to aid us — and he agreed that it was a good idea. We parted from each other at the N.T.C., he going ahead to Stanton Street to fix things up and I was to follow in my car later on. My idea, after Claire had called at Stanton Street, was to drive her home — '

'Yes, yes, go on!' Garth waved a hand impatiently.

'I arrived at Stanton Street about seven-fifteen and was surprised to find Cliff Brand there too. He had not joined Leslie and me before at the house because he didn't want his association with the place to be known in case it leaked out that he was financing it. It appeared that Les Carson had called on him at his salon, told him of my intentions — all in good faith — and he had arrived to play the devil. And *how* he played it!

'He was already in a bad temper after knowing old man Hammond had turned me down the night before — and when he knew that in spite of everything I intended to demonstrate the invention to Claire he raised the roof. He wanted to know *why?* Since Hammond was not going to help, why should he even have an inkling, through his daughter, of what was going on? Cliff Brand said he had other big moneyed men in mind who'd help us. He did not know I'd fallen in love with Claire and he was determined she should not know a thing . . . '

Harvey sighed. 'Well, he being the money-bags, I was more or less compelled to heed him. He didn't say I wasn't to mention Stanton Street or deny to Claire that I had sent that letter, but I was *not* to let her see the invention or allow her in the house.'

Harvey sat considering, his brows knitted.

'In a fury I left the house,' he continued presently. 'I went for a drive in my car — as far as Montrose's Drive-In Café on the Redhill main road. Just then I could think of no plan to explain things to Claire, and it was too late to contact her. I decided to let her manage whilst I thought out what to do next. As I drove out of Stanton Street I saw her, but ignored her. By the time I saw her again, at my flat, she rightly upbraided me, but by then I had made up my mind to tell her everything, Cliff or no Cliff. I did intend to — '

'And a telephone call made you change your mind?' Garth asked, coming back to the starting-point. 'Was it from Brand? I might as well tell you that he has as good as admitted it to me — albeit unintentionally.

'Yes — it was Cliff Brand,' Harvey admitted warily.

'I'm not sure of what he said, Mr. Dell, but I'll lay evens he told you what happened to Hammond. You got the shock of your life in consequence and suddenly became so utterly secretive that there was no getting a word out of you.'

'He told me that Mr. Hammond had come chasing after his daughter,' Harvey responded. 'That he had arrived only a few minutes after he — Brand — had done his best to convince Claire that she had made a mistake and been turned away. An argument sprang up between Les Carson and Hammond and in the process Les struck Hammond a blow on the head with a heavy wrench, which killed him. *Why* it killed him Cliff did not seem to know because the blow had not been a very heavy one. Anyway, Les was frightened to death because it was murder.'

'Then what?' Garth snapped.

'Cliff told me that Les had made arrangements to get rid of Hammond's body so the police could never solve how it came to be where it eventually turned up. Then Les, a fugitive, escaped. As his friend, I was in a frightful mess. I didn't want to conceal the identity of the murderer of the father of the girl I loved — yet on the other hand I didn't want to tell the police that one of my best friends was the killer. So between the two issues I resolved to keep quiet.'

'You ignore certain vital details with disagreeable ease,' Garth commented, his eyes cold. 'You say that Leslie Carson had made arrangements to get rid of the body . . . *What* arrangements?'

'I don't know. I never saw him alive again to ask him.'

'What you really mean is that you know perfectly well what he did, but you've no intention of telling me?'

'I've already told you a good deal,' Harvey retorted. 'But I certainly won't reveal secrets which it has taken me years to discover. That way I stand to lose a fortune. I just daren't tell you what I know, but I do swear to you that I had nothing to do with Mr. Hammond's death, or his removal to Worthing.'

'You have spoken of enemies,' Garth said slowly. 'I take it you were always on the alert for that possibility?'

'If you've invented something of tremendous importance you just have to take precautions.'

'And these precautions were put into effect not because of enemies but because a man — Hammond — had been murdered? I refer to the empty house, the dust, the vanishing curtains . . . '

Harvey smiled faintly. 'Everything in that house was so planned that it could be removed at a second's notice. The light in the front room was put there to assure people outside that the house was lived in whilst we actually worked in the basement. As for the dust, that was Carson's idea. Simply a hand-operated bellows with a dust-bag of which he gave all of us a demonstration one day at Cliff Brand's home: I remember how he made a row about the mess it made. Escape was made down the shaft on a collapsible ladder, which was always in position when we were busy. A rowboat did the rest. It was always anchored in readiness . . . You see, to give the impression that the house had never been used — despite the front-room light — would fool *any* enemy who tried to start tracing us. As it happened our enemy became the law, on the death of Hammond.'

'Was it Carson or Brand who finished off the details? Who removed everything, laid the dust, and tipped your turbo-generator and a good deal of equipment into the stream?'

'Brand told me over the phone that Carson was going to do all that, and I supposed that he did. The news of his 'disappearance' was no surprise to me. The surprise came when I learned that he had been strangled.'

'I gathered that,' Garth commented. 'I had suspected that the reason for your silence was because you were shielding somebody — but when I told you that Carson had been murdered I anticipated that you'd stop trying to be evasive, for your own sake. I guessed wrong . . . Isn't it time you loosened up still more, Mr. Dell?'

'But I don't know who *could* have murdered him, Inspector! It certainly wasn't Cliff Brand, if that's what you are thinking. No man would murder the goose which laid the golden eggs.'

'Meaning what?' Garth snapped.

'The three of us — Les Carson, Brand, and myself — formed a triumvirate,' Harvey said. 'Carson was the scientific engineer, the man who could translate any blueprint into actual fact. I was the brains behind the actual design. Les and I together were perfect: apart, I had the idea but no constructional knowledge of engineering: he had the power to construct but no genius for thinking of something *to* construct. And Cliff Brand provided the money. So, with Carson gone, Brand and I are both left high and dry, so to speak.'

'There are other scientific engineers in the world,' Garth said.

'Maybe — but which dare we trust? An invention like mine demands a life-long friend such as Les Carson was. Brand would never murder him: it would cut his own throat.'

'What about James Mitchell, of Lancing?' Garth asked quietly.

'You mentioned him before,' Harvey said. 'When you were at the Hammond place. He simply happened to be a friend of Les Carson's.'

'And not a friend of yours, or Brand's?' Garth raised a hand before Harvey could answer. 'Think carefully, Mr. Dell! Mitchell has a hut full of peculiar electrical apparatus and it happened to be the nearest building to Mr. Hammond when his body was found on the Worthing road. If there is a connection between you, him, and Brand, you'd better admit it.'

Harvey shrugged. 'That Mitchell happens to have a hut full of electrical stuff which was near Hammond's body is purely coincidental, I'd say. He was chiefly a friend of Leslie's, though. I knew him because at one time he worked in the laboratories of the War Office. Later he turned to scientific agriculture.'

'With ham radio as a hobby?' Garth questioned.

'Yes, so I believe. Anyway, if you are thinking that maybe he killed Les Carson you're off your horse again. He couldn't have because he was in Lancing that evening.'

'How do you know?'

'Because when he rang me up, Cliff Brand told me that he had been through to Lancing to tell Jimmy Mitchell what had happened. Jimmy being Leslie's friend, Cliff Brand thought he ought to know the facts in case Les, on the run, tried to get in touch with him. Since Jimmy was in Lancing, sixty miles away, and Leslie's body was found in the Thames, Jimmy could hardly be the culprit, could he? And anyway, what on earth could have been his motive?'

Garth smiled faintly, as if to himself. Then he changed the subject.

'And this invention of yours, Mr. Dell? You are determined not to tell me what it is, aren't you?'

'Yes. It's too dangerous to reveal anything about it until I know exactly where I stand.'

'Well, having eliminated Brand and

Mitchell as the possible murderers of Leslie Carson — to your own satisfaction, anyway — who do you think might have killed him?'

'I've known for some time that certain factions had tried to pump Leslie for information. He was less guarded than I. He had let something slip about the invention and listening ears had picked it up. I think that, in escaping, he may have run into these enemies and, in refusing them any information, got himself murdered. That's the best guess I can make.'

'Murder by person or persons unknown?' Garth rubbed his chest slowly and meditated. 'Your invention — or part of it — was found in the bed of the underground stream . . . '

'Possibly. Les Carson threw it there down the shaft, I expect, together with the turbo-generator. But he wouldn't be fool enough to leave vital parts to be found.'

'He didn't. Dr. Carruthers was quite annoyed when he found that out.'

Harvey started. 'You mean 'Tea-pot' Caruthers, the ex-boffin? How on earth

274

does he fit into this business?'

'Dr. Carruthers told me that he was acquainted with you from your work as a scientist for the government,' Garth responded. 'These days, he is ostensibly retired, but we at the Yard here call on his services now and again when we hit a problem which baffles us because of its apparent scientific implication. When that happens, Dr. Carruthers steps in. Right now he is trying to piece together the parts of the apparatus fished from the stream. And knowing him, he'll succeed!'

Harvey Dell was silent, biting his lower lip.

'So you see, Mr. Dell, in time the whole thing will be sorted out. The missing parts no longer signify. The design of that mysterious invention of yours was in your safe, wasn't it?'

Harvey looked up angrily. 'You mean you *copied* it? You hadn't the time!'

'Micro-camera. I'm surprised at you, a scientist, overlooking such a simple thing.'

'So, invading my flat under the cover of a search warrant, you photographed my invention design and handed it to one of

the cleverest scientists in the country! You
stop at nothing, do you, Inspector?'

'Not when I want results, Mr. Dell.
You've only yourself to blame. But
Scotland Yard or Dr. Carruthers will not
steal your idea, if that's what you're afraid
of.'

'You're clever, Inspector: I've noticed
the neat way in which you trick people
into making unwary statements. How do
I know you're not bluffing? If, on the
strength of that bluff, I told you all
you want to know, I'd be crazy. So, if you
don't mind I'll be going!'

Garth's pale eyes followed Harvey as
he moved to the door. 'I'll be seeing you
again before long.' He got to his feet,
poured himself a brandy and soda, drank
it, and rumbled satanically.

'Caution, with that bloke, amounts to a
disease,' he mused. 'As for Leslie Carson
— as if there could any longer be any
doubt as to who did it, or for why.
Funny how some people give themselves
away . . .'

14

When Whittaker returned, towards half past eight, he reported that the eccentric Carruthers had promised that he would telephone the moment he had anything worthwhile to say. Apparently it would take him some days to secure the extra parts he needed, or to make them himself.

To Garth the idea of waiting for days was exasperating, particularly with the chief constable and assistant commissioner breathing down his neck. Whittaker, in his turn, heard all the details of Dell's visit. What he thought of the issue he did not say. Like Garth, however, his main preoccupation was that of wondering what kind of an invention Harvey Dell could have . . .

Several days passed. Leslie Carson was buried, Dell and Brand both being present at the funeral. Garth did his best to stall the powers-that-be — then on the

Tuesday in mid-morning, the following week, there came a cryptic phone message ordering Garth to Halingford to see something 'quite intriguing'.

He wasted no time in complying and took Whittaker with him. It was Mrs. Barret who opened the door to them. She was as immovable as ever.

'Good morning, Inspector — Sergeant. The doctor is in his laboratory.' She closed the front door. 'I'll take — '

'I know — the door let into the staircase,' Garth said, striding forward 'Don't take up your time, Mrs. Barret.'

He opened the door and led the way down a flight of wooden steps into a brilliantly lighted basement, its floor made of concrete and the walls yellow-distempered. Whittaker, who had never been down here before, gazed about him in amazement. Equipment and benches seemed to be everywhere, and there were enough switch-panels and variously sized generators to run a small powerhouse.

In the midst of all this impedimenta the vest-pocket scientist in his old jacket and trousers was screwing up the end of a long cable into a massive plug.

'About time you got here,' he growled, raising his eyes for a moment as the two men walked over to him.

'Well, I like that!' Garth snapped. 'You take four days to do something and then blame us for being late!'

'I was delayed in getting the material for the missing parts,' Carruthers said. 'Once I did get it I made the stuff myself. It's more or less makeshift but it should do for our job. I've had to work pretty nearly night and day. Those inductance coils had the most complicated wirings.' He finished screwing the plug on the cable and walked with it to a tall, stand-like machine of slender outlines in a clear space a few yards away. Garth looked at it and frowned.

'Just a moment, doctor! I recognize that huge magnet. Is that the original apparatus, built up?

'Naturally. Thanks to that print you sent me I've been able to rebuild the whole thing, part for part, connection for connection. It's as I thought — Harvey Dell is a genius. Little wonder he's been guarding his idea with everything he's got.'

'What *is* the contraption, sir?' Whittaker asked.

'Radio equipment of an entirely revolutionary design — but its exact purpose I haven't yet solved . . . ' Carruthers stood back from the equipment.

'The central part of the whole thing is this magnet,' he said, nodding to it. 'That magnet absorbs electrons — just as an ordinary magnet attracts steel particles. It isn't an ordinary magnet, however. The electrons it absorbs pass into its substance, through its interstices.' Carruthers stopped and grinned insolently. 'Bet I'm getting too clever for you, eh?'

'We went to school!' Garth retorted. 'By 'interstices' I suppose you mean the invisible holes which exist throughout all matter?'

'*Holes!*' Carruthers almost jumped. 'He calls the inter-atomic spaces between molecular clusters *holes*! No wonder civilization is at a standstill!'

'Skip the insults,' Garth said grimly. 'What happens when the electrons have been absorbed into the substance of the magnet? I take it you mean that it absorbs electrons as a sponge absorbs water?'

'For that gleam of light in a dark Age, many thanks,' Carruthers acknowledged. 'Yes, that's what I *do* mean. The electrons thus absorbed are transmitted to this transformer here' — he tapped a square and not over-large object with a little grating let into the metal side — 'and there they undergo a kind of what I would call *binding* process.'

'Is that the transformer which was missing from the set-up?' the chief inspector questioned.

'Yes. And no wonder it was missing! It gathers electrons and atomic patterns into itself and forms them into one compact mass of energy — rather in the same way as a machine can thresh, sort, and bind wheat.'

Carruthers's slender hands indicated other parts of the complicated apparatus.

'The 'energy-pack', as I'll call it, is next transferred through these inductance coils and rectifiers and eventually enters this chamber here . . . ' He pointed to a semitransparent perspex affair like an oblong cellophane box. 'From this it passes to this transmitter, which is actually a small-scale version of a normal radio transmitter — beam-type, not wave.'

Garth's was struggling. 'By 'beam' do you mean something like radar beams?'

'Well, yes,' Carruthers agreed. 'But radar is old-fashioned compared to this. By a beam I don't mean something that comes from lime or searchlight. It's invisible. It's a beam of pure energy, which, like all radio waves, will pass through solids. Only it is a beam in that it points in one fixed direction instead of dispersing in ever-expanding waves of energy . . . In the old days of radio the expanding wave system was the only system, if you remember. Later came the direct beam transmission system. Then came this!'

'Okay. You mean it transmits radio in a straight invisible beam through solids to . . . ' Garth stopped and frowned. 'To where?'

'Anywhere the operator selects,' the scientist replied.

'Then beyond the fact that it is a queer-fangled radio you don't know much more about it?'

'I shall when I find the companion machine to it,' Carruthers said. Wandering across to a nearby bench, he pushed aside a toolbox, and brought an aluminium teapot in a knitted cosy into view. He half-filled a cup and swallowed the tepid muck slowly as he pondered.

'Companion machine?' Garth repeated. He thought for a moment, then snapped his fingers. 'If this apparatus has a receiver somewhere it'll be in Lancing. And owned by Jimmy Mitchell, I'll bet!'

'I wondered if you would finally come round to that,' Carruthers murmured, nodding. 'Yes. Obviously since Mitchell has a shed full of what looks like radio equipment — to the uninitiated, that is — and he was nearest to Hammond when he was found, *and* is a friend of Harvey Dell, or at least connected with him, the companion-piece to this equipment lies in Lancing. And that,' Carruthers finished, putting down the teapot, 'is where we are going this moment.'

Fifteen minutes later, he, Garth and Whittaker were in a compartment to themselves in a south-coast-bound train. Carruthers sat brooding in a corner seat, his Homburg on the back of his wild mane of hair and the collar of his gigantic overcoat turned up round his ears.

'If ever there was an involved way of committing a murder, this is it.' Garth declared at length.

Carruthers glanced at him. 'You don't suppose that equipment was used to murder Hammond, do you? A scientist brilliant enough to invent a thing like that wouldn't use it to kill a man and then chuck the remains in a stream. That instrument had nothing to do with the murder — as such. Hammond died because of a blow on the head with a wrench — or so Dell told you. The blow wasn't heavy, apparently, but Hammond's queer bone disease made the blow fatal.'

'If Carson, Dell, and Brand didn't know about Mr. Hammond's bone trouble,' Whittaker said slowly, 'no wonder there was panic.'

Garth considered the wintry countryside. 'Dell *did* know. But as far as I know, Carson and Brand did not . . . Y'know, what that apparatus *did* do, I think, was smash every bone in Hammond's body and transfer certain of his internal organs. What do you think of that, Doctor?'

'Possible,' Carruthers conceded; then he moved irritably. 'But all this amounts to mere theory. Let's get the facts first, first-hand in Lancing if we can. Certainly I have wondered about those misplaced internal organs and shattered bones ever since you mentioned them — and I am inclined to think that that apparatus had a lot to do with it. If so, then take it from me, whether Hammond had suffered from *fragilitas* or not, his bones would probably have *still* been broken when he was found . . . '

Further than this he refused to go, and for the rest of the journey to the south coast he remained lost in speculations.

It was lunchtime when they finally arrived in Worthing. After finding a café and partaking of a quick meal they set off for police headquarters. Inspector Grimshaw seemed surprised but nonetheless pleased to see them.

'Mitchell?' he repeated, when Garth had made clear the purpose of the visit. 'So you've come round to him, have you?'

'Inevitably,' Garth responded. 'I know that you interviewed him and found his hut with the 'ham' radio stuff in it — but matters don't end there. In fact, Mitchell looks as though he might be the last link in a remarkably complicated chain.'

'All right, let's be going,' Grimshaw said, putting on his uniform cap, 'my car's at the door. You stay here in charge, Sergeant,' he added, to the man at the desk in the corner.

The four men left the office and Grimshaw himself took the wheel. He soon had the car streaking along the main coast road from Worthing to Lancing, then at one point about half a mile from Lancing he slowed to a stop and nodded through the window to a solitary hut on the downland side of the road. Behind it ranged the downs themselves, marred here and there by the ugly bulks of steel power-pylons.

'That's Mitchell's hut,' Grimshaw said. 'Hammond's body was found just about here on the road.'

'Nothing to be gained by looking at the hut from the outside,' Carruthers snorted. 'X-ray eyesight is something I leave to Superman — Carry on to wherever we find this chap Mitchell.'

'At the farm a mile farther,' Grimshaw said, slipping in the first gear again. He did not add any more. Carruthers's remark had rather deflated him.

The remaining mile was covered and Grimshaw turned the car off the main road and down a rough side lane, which finished its course at two very modern-looking iron gates. On them was a sign — KEEP OUT! — and beyond them a farm of newly erected white buildings, extensive yards, and all the signs of highly modernized agriculture.

'This is an experimental farm,' Grimshaw remarked, sounding the horn. 'Probably more for research than anything else.'

In response to the horn a man presently appeared from a little glass-housed affair like a sentry box. He was in a uniform and peaked uniform cap with an armband having the initials G.H.S.R. inscribed upon it.

''Government Holding for Scientific Research',' Garth interpreted. 'Quite a lot of them these days — '

'Well, what is it?' the man demanded; then his attitude changed as he recognized Grimshaw looking at him through the car's open side-window.

'Remember me? Open up, please!'

The order was obeyed and the gatekeeper followed the car into the broad yard. Garth clambered out. 'I'm Inspector; Garth, C.I.D.,' he explained. 'Where can I contact Mr. James Mitchell?'

The gatekeeper jerked his head and the four men followed him across the yard to a low-built, white-painted annex with many windows. He opened the door and motioned inside. 'You'll find Mr. Mitchell in here, Inspector,' he said, and turned away.

Garth entered the building and stood

looking about him. It was extremely long and had the appearance of a doctor's surgery, except that the 'patients' composed hens behind wire-netting, pigs in pens, and white mice scuttling about small wired-front boxes. At the benches by the windows, littered with scientific instruments and binocular-microscopes, both men and women in white overalls were at work, making notes, studying slides, and doing a variety of tasks. They ignored the visitors.

'There's Mitchell,' Grimshaw said quietly, and nodded to a young man with broad shoulders, unusual copper-colored hair, and somewhat fleshy features. As Grimshaw went up to him he glanced from his work and gave a start of surprise.

'You again, Inspector?' Mitchell readily came forward to where the others were standing. There was a frank openness in his face and blue eyes.

Garth showed his warrant card. 'I'd like a few words with you about that hut of yours, Mr. Mitchell.'

Mitchell gave a rather wondering smile. 'Look here, what *is* all this about my hut? I've already explained everything to the inspector here when he interviewed me.'

'Just the same I would still like to see that hut. We'll drive there now.'

'I — I have some work to finish . . . '

'It can wait,' Garth said calmly. 'The law isn't asking you to come, sir: it's telling you!'

Mitchell shrugged and went across to a locker. He rid himself of his white overall and got into a jacket and overcoat then he accompanied the four men from the laboratory and across the yard to the car. Grimshaw drove them back to the point on the main road nearest the hut. In a body they climbed up the grass bank and walked over the damp, sandy soil to where the hut stood. Mitchell fumbled in his pocket for keys. As he hesitated, Garth said:

'This is purely routine, Mr. Mitchell. Scotland Yard is investigating the mysterious death of Mr. Hammond so I'm checking up on all points in the case.'

Mitchell hesitated no longer. Finishing the job of unlocking the padlock, he flung the hut door wide open. Reaching inside he snapped a switch on the rough wooden wall and the dimness of the interior — the windows being blocked with stout planking — became banished by a string of three moderately powerful lamps.

Garth walked into the hut slowly, surveying. The floor, walls and ceiling — or rather the roof, since it went up to a triangle apex — were all of wood. Overhead there seemed to be multitudes of wires. Against the walls were benches and panels containing dials and meters. A single bentwood chair seemed to be the only article of furniture. Carruthers, his eyes sharp, glanced in various directions whilst Garth moved his attention back to Mitchell.

'How do you happen to have these lights?' he inquired. 'No power laid on, is there?'

'Batteries in series,' Mitchell responded. 'When I want to charge them up I take them to the farm in my car. There are chargers there I can use any time I want.'

Garth's pale eyes strayed again to the

panels, mysterious antennae and cage-aerials, small dynamos in odd corners, loudspeakers, headphones, a small Morse spark-transmitter, an old gramophone dual-turntable . . .

'I understand,' Garth said, without looking at Mitchell, 'that you are a 'ham' radio fan?'

'I'm a rabid one. I told the inspector as much.'

'And all this apparatus, young man, is radio reception and transmission equipment?' Carruthers asked abruptly, coming to life after a long survey. 'How wide an area do you cover in your transmission?'

'Oh, anything up to fifty miles.'

'On batteries?'

Silence. Mitchell stood frowning.

'Don't waste your time answering,' Carruthers said, waving a hand. 'You couldn't do it on batteries. Not enough juice. However, I do notice that in a corner there you have two drums of cable which, judging from the careless way they have been wound, have been used a good deal. I also notice the large crocodile-clips on each cable.' Carruthers grinned disarmingly. 'Just about enough cable there to clip on the power lines about quarter of a mile away, eh?'

Mitchell coloured. 'Are you suggesting I pirate power from the overhead lines?'

'I'm not suggesting; I'm telling you that you do, because in the absence of any other form of power — turbo-generator for instance — you couldn't do otherwise.'

Mitchell's face became ugly and it was a surprising transformation from the amiable smile he had had. 'Who are you to come poking and prying,' he snapped. 'The police I can't stop, but who are *you*?'

'Hiram Carruthers,' the little physicist answered. 'If you are anything of a scientist you've heard of me.'

A vague look of consternation crossed Mitchell's face.

Carruthers strolled forward, and prowled about the hut. At last he turned and looked at Grimshaw. 'Is this place the same as when you first examined it, Inspector?'

'In the main details, yes,' Grimshaw

agreed. 'I can't pretend to know whether every dial and instrument — '

Carruthers cut him short. 'When you first looked in here, the day after Hammond was found, did you notice anything resembling a large horseshoe? Say, about seven feet high, very thin, with the feet about five feet apart?'

'There was nothing like that,' Grimshaw replied, perfectly sure of himself.

'In other words, there was plenty of time to move away the most significant apparatus,' Carruthers said, and his gaze shifted to Mitchell.

'I don't know what in blazes you're talking about!' the young man objected hotly.

Carruthers eyed him. 'Yes you do. For one thing you are *not* a 'ham' radio fan. My home is in Halingford, thirty miles from here. I'm a 'ham' myself: do quite a lot of it, and I know most of the other chaps within a fifty-mile radius by their first names. I never heard of you or your call-sign in all my life.'

'I've a licence to transmit and receive!'

'What does that prove?' Carruthers

snorted. 'You are not compelled to transmit and receive just because you have a licence. That's a plain cover up.'

'When was the licence taken out?' Garth asked, looking at Grimshaw.

'This summer. It expires thirtieth of June next year.'

'June,' Garth mused. 'The month when this whole affair began to take shape. Ties up nicely. Sorry, Doc — carry on.'

Carruthers said deliberately: 'For an amateur radio station like this is supposed to be you don't need equipment as complicated or as expensive as this. Nor do you need all these switch-panels to show variations of current and radio-beam direction. This oscillograph here alone is worth a packet . . . I'll tell you what you have done, Mitchell. You've left in the basic radio equipment because of difficulty in dismantling it, but you have removed more obvious parts — namely, a specially built transformer, a group of three inductance coils, and the big horseshoe magnet I referred to. Where are they?'

'I don't know what you're talking

about,' Mitchell insisted.

'Listen to me, young man,' Carruthers said, coming forward with menace in his eyes. 'Don't you realize just how serious this whole business is? I know perfectly well what you have been up to — in collusion with Harvey Dell, Clifton Brand, and Leslie Carson, the late. The fact remains that here in this hut there should be a duplicate of an apparatus which existed in 9 Stanton Street, London, before it was quickly dismantled and parts of it destroyed.'

'Not much use holding out when the rest of the party has given up the ghost, is it?' Garth asked. 'Harvey Dell gave me all the facts last night. That's why I'm here.'

'You mean he *split* on me?' An ugly look came back to Mitchell's face.

'All right! Why the devil should I be left holding the baby? That horseshoe magnet and transformer and odds and ends you're looking for are in an old copper mineshaft about two miles from here. I threw them down there so nobody would ever find 'em.'

'All right,' Garth said. 'You can show us

the spot later. What's the meaning of this apparatus?'

'I don't see why I should tell you about this apparatus,' Mitchell said obstinately. 'At least not until I'm sure that Harvey Dell has given away his secret amongst other things. I cannot think that he would give that away no matter how many other things he may have revealed.'

'Son, you don't have to say anything!' Carruthers declared. 'I know the answer without your aid — and the sooner we get to that copper mine the better!'

Garth reflected, then took the little scientist on one side. 'Do you suppose that I ought to arrest him on a charge of conspiracy? I ought to, after he has admitted so much.'

'Don't be a fool,' the physicist answered, keeping his voice low. 'This young man has been swept up in the midst of a terrible, unprecedented accident. Certainly I'm convinced that he didn't commit murder.'

'Okay,' Garth nodded. 'Maybe we'll get more out of him by doing nothing. But if you're wrong, Doctor, I'm liable to wind up as P.C. Garth.'

Carruthers grinned contemptuously. 'Whoever heard of me being wrong?' He resumed his normal tone. 'Come on, young man! Let's be going!'

Mitchell nodded and accompanied the men out of the hut, locking the padlock securely behind him. 'I take it,' he said, as they all walked across the field to the car, 'that I am not under arrest?'

'Not at the moment,' Garth responded, and inwardly felt uncertain of his judgment. 'But you have laid yourself open to arrest by obstructing justice.'

He reflected that Harvey Dell and Clifton Brand, and now Mitchell, should all have been arrested for misdemeanor — but with all of them thus nailed where would there be a chance to get at the real problem — the murders of Hammond and Carson, and particularly the incredible transition of the former after his death?

15

Towards mid-afternoon, with Mitchell directing operations, the immense slender horseshoe magnet and the missing transformer and inductance coils had all been recovered from the mineshaft. Carruthers duly examined them and pronounced himself satisfied. 'You can go home now,' he told Mitchell. 'Or don't you know when you're well off?'

Mitchell hesitated briefly, then hurried away across the rough, wintry landscape.

'I don't like it,' Garth insisted. 'He ought to be put under arrest!'

Carruthers grinned. 'What do you think he'll do now that he knows we — or rather I — am so completely conversant with his little game? Do you think he'll just go home quietly? Like hell! Since he knows Dell and Brand are still free he will tell one or other of them that the secret isn't going to last much longer — and since you were only bluffing Mitchell in

299

saying Dell had confessed, he — or Brand — is going to have the wind up. From the reactions of Dell or Brand, you should be able to judge if either of them had anything to do with the murder of Hammond or Carson.'

'Subtle,' Grimshaw smiled. 'If a trifle unorthodox.'

'But didn't Leslie Carson kill Hammond?' Whittaker asked.

'I don't think he did,' Garth responded, 'and later I'll tell you why I think that. Even if he did, we still want to know who took care of *him* . . . I see your point, Doctor, and it's a good one.'

'Naturally,' the physicist agreed. 'You have two men watching the movements of Dell and Brand, you say, and their telephones are tapped — so nothing will reach either of them from Mitchell without you knowing it. Now, give me a hand with this stuff back to the car. I want to get it to Mitchell's hut. And if the padlock worries you it needn't. I've got keys that would open the Bank of England if necessary.'

Garth said: 'It's contrary to law — '

'For you, maybe, but I don't represent the law. I'm a private citizen and you can arrest me for trespass any time you wish.'

'All right,' Garth growled. 'So you're going to work in the shed. What then?'

'I want two constables, Inspector, to stand guard over the place — with reliefs of course — until further notice,' Carruthers instructed. 'I need protection. In about two or three days I hope to have something definite for you.'

'You mean you'll be able to explain what happened to Hammond?'

'You bet I will! Now give me a hand to the car with this stuff.'

The little physicist's order was obeyed, and the last Garth, Whittaker, and Grimshaw saw of him was his active, gnome-like figure in the hut as he took off his gigantic overcoat and prepared to get down to work. Just the same Grimshaw took no chances. Whilst Garth and Whittaker remained outside the hut on guard, the inspector telephoned his headquarters for two constables. Only when they had arrived to stand guard did he drive back to Worthing with Whittaker and Garth.

'And what happens now, sir?' he asked, as they entered his office.

'I want to borrow your car — or a car,' Garth said. 'I've been thinking — whilst I'm in the vicinity I'd better call at that drive-in café Harvey Dell said he called at on the night of the crime. Just to verify it. Have to go by road for that. The sergeant can drive your car back to you tomorrow.'

Grimshaw raised no objections and in a few minutes, Whittaker at the wheel, the car was on its way. Finally they came upon Montrose's Drive-in Café on the main Redhill road. Whittaker drew the car in to the cinder park.

'Shan't need you for this,' Garth said, climbing out. 'Be back in a moment.'

He entered the café's well-lighted interior to find it empty save for the proprietor. The tables were polished and waiting — somewhat forlornly. The proprietor brisked up as he scented business, however small.

Garth displayed his warrant card. 'I'd like some information from you, sir

— You are the proprietor, I suppose?'

'Yes. I'm Montrose.'

'Good. I'm making some inquiries about a Mr. Harvey Dell. Do you know him?'

Montrose stared. 'Yes, certainly I do. He often comes in here — or he did do. Drives up and down a lot in his car between London and Lancing.'

'Was he here at about ten to nine a week ago tonight?'

The proprietor reflected. 'Last Tuesday — ? Why yes, he was!' he exclaimed suddenly. 'He said he was thinking of driving through to Lancing, and then before he left he changed his mind and decided to go back home. The weather had turned out filthy, if you remember. He said his trip was not so important that it was worth driving in such stuff — or words to that effect.'

'Thanks,' Garth said quietly. 'Much obliged.'

He left and returned to the car. Whittaker looked at him in the glow from the dashboard. 'It checks,' Garth said. 'Carry on — straight to London.'

Whittaker had driven five miles on the almost deserted road, the headlamps blazing, before he spoke. 'If Dell did stop there, he travelled in the same direction as the body,' he mused.

'As far as I am concerned,' Garth responded, relaxing and giving a broad grin, 'those few words with the café proprietor have satisfied me beyond a doubt as to who murdered Hammond and Carson, and for why. I've got the last links, Whitty, as far as my side is concerned. The rest is up to that crackpot genius with the teapot . . . '

★   ★   ★

Garth arrived back at his office with the expectancy of discovering some news concerning the activity of Mitchell, but in this he was disappointed.

The chief inspector threw himself in the swivel chair and glanced at the clock. It was half past six. 'Should be a report of some kind soon,' he commented. 'I'll hang around just in case — Better order some tea Whitty.'

Whittaker nodded and went out. In ten minutes the tea had arrived. Whittaker busied himself with the pot. 'Why are you still worrying about what Mitchell does,' he remarked, handing over a cup. 'You say you know the murderer — so there is nothing Mitchell can do to alter that, is there?'

'Not alter it, but he can perhaps confirm it,' Garth explained, stirring the tea slowly. 'I can only see one possible culprit for both murders — but then I'm not infallible. If Mitchell does tell either Dell or Brand how far we've got to finding out the truth, the logical possibility is that either Dell or Brand will try and escape — and quickly. If that happens it will verify my suspicions. I'm not doing anything until I'm absolutely sure.'

'Do you think,' Whittaker asked, munching a sandwich, 'that Mitchell knows who is responsible for the murders?'

'I've no idea. If Carruthers is to be believed Mitchell is simply a catspaw in the whole thing, in which case he *won't* know who's responsible — '

Garth put down his teacup hastily and picked up the shrilling telephone.

'Yes? Garth speaking.'

'Walters here, sir,' a voice responded. 'There's a phone call just been made to Harvey Dell's flat from somebody calling himself Jimmy. We made an instantaneous recording of it. Here it is. If you'll just listen . . . '

Garth held the receiver more tightly to his ear and munched a sandwich as he listened to the somewhat tinny playback.

'Hallo — hallo — That you, Harvey? This is Jimmy.'

'Jimmy? What the devil do you want to use the phone for? Don't you realize that the police may be keeping the lines tapped? I'm pretty heavily under suspicion as it is. What's the matter?'

'You ask *me* that?' There was anger in Mitchell's voice. 'You go and shoot your face off to the police about me and everything else, and then you ask me what's wrong? I had to take this risk to phone you. They're on to everything. They have got 'Teapot' Carruthers putting your invention together!'

'I know that. Inspector Garth told me as much, but as long as the vital parts of the receiver are kept out of sight Carruthers can't do a thing. The design for the receiver is safely tucked away in the bank at the moment, otherwise that sleuth-hound Garth would have photographed it as he did that of the transmitter . . . And what do you mean by my shooting my face off? I haven't said anything yet that really matters. If I had do you think I'd be walking around free?'

'You mean that?' Mitchell gasped in consternation. 'But I was led to think otherwise — so much so that I didn't see why I should be left holding the baby. I — I gave Carruthers the missing parts.'

'You what?' Harvey yelled.

'I had to. Since it seemed that you'd told everything there wasn't any point in my holding out, though I didn't tell anything about the invention. I thought you hadn't been such an idiot as to give that away.'

'You might just as well have done so since you handed over the missing parts! You damned idiot! Carruthers will patch up the whole thing in no time.'

'I couldn't do anything else. I had bobbies around me and I was under the threat of arrest — I thought you'd split on me so I gave up trying to be careful.'

'Some friend you turned out to be!' Harvey shouted. 'All right, I'll take care of this . . . '

The recording clicked and there was silence. Garth stirred, his eyes hard.

'Walters, has Dell made any phone calls besides getting this one?' he asked.

'No, sir. We're keeping close watch. We have this recording van near his flat — and another one using short-wave is tapping the phone lines. Men are also watching Brand's home and salon. Another man is watching the N.T.C. and has a tap on the line there — '

'Has Dell left his flat?'

'No, he . . . ' Walters broke off. 'Just a minute, sir. He's leaving the building now!'

'Don't lose him,' Garth ordered. 'Radio the nearest squad car and have them keep watch on him. Follow him wherever he goes: my guess is he may take out his car and go to Lancing. Report back to me the moment you have information.'

Garth put his finger on the phone cradle for a moment and then removed it.

'Get me Worthing police headquarters — and hurry it up!'

He waited, watching Whittaker across the desk. The sergeant had heard everything and subdued interest was mirrored on his square face.

'Grimshaw?' Garth asked, coming to attention as the receiver squawked. 'Garth here. I believe Harvey Dell may be on his way to Lancing, and he'll either go and see Jimmy Mitchell, or else he'll make straight for that hut and do his best to smash the apparatus — and maybe Carruthers with it. Double the guard and take charge yourself. The moment you can apprehend Dell, detain him at headquarters and advise me. Get Mitchell as well. Book them on charges of obstruction.'

'Right, sir,' the inspector promised, and rang off.

'You seem pretty sure what Harvey

Dell is going to do, sir,' Whittaker commented.

'I am! He'll go to any length to stop that invention of his being pieced together, because once it is, the secret and a possible fortune is out of his hands; and for another thing the mystery of what happened to Hammond will be a mystery no longer. He's not going to succeed because we're too wary for him. With him detained by the Worthing police he'll be out of the picture — as will Mitchell — and Carruthers will be able to finish his job in peace. As for me, I've work to do . . . '

Garth got to his feet and hurried into his hat and coat. Whittaker looked at him questioningly. 'I want to ask Clifton Brand a few more questions,' the chief inspector explained. 'You'd better come with me: I'm going to need you.'

* * *

Some little time later Whittaker drove the police car into the most fashionable quarter of Hampstead and drew up

310

outside an old-fashioned residence with big stone gates.

'This is Brand's place all right,' Garth muttered, peering at the gateposts in the dim light. 'Nineteen Fenway Road . . . Okay, let's have a word with him.'

Whittaker nodded, though he could not fathom his superior's purpose in visiting Clifton Brand when Harvey Dell was at this moment probably driving hell-bent for the south coast. He walked beside his superior up the long, dim drive to the front door of the house. A maid opened the door in response to Garth's steady ringing.

'Mr. Clifton Brand at home?' Garth asked briefly. 'I'm Inspector Garth, from the C.I.D.'

'I — er . . . ' The maid hesitated and then glanced behind her as a voice spoke. An extremely tall figure was coming down the broad staircase.

'Who is it, Ellen? Somebody to see me?'

Garth stepped into the hall with Whittaker behind him. Brand came forward in some surprise. He was wearing a quilted dressing gown over his shirt and striped trousers.

'Inspector Garth — and the sergeant!' he exclaimed.

He motioned into the lounge and languidly followed the two men in. The big room was quietly comfortable with its bright lighting and a glowing fire. Garth glanced about him, satisfied that nobody else was present, then he turned to Brand as he strolled forward after closing the door.

'Well, gentlemen, what can I do for you?' The smile on his darkly handsome face was faintly cynical. He took his cigarette case from his dressing gown and extended it. Garth shook his head.

'No, thanks . . . And I must apologize for coming here without a prior appointment.'

Brand's smile deepened but hard lights were in his dark eyes. 'You police have a habit of bursting in suddenly on people, haven't you? Sit down, please.'

Garth moved to a chair and relaxed in it. Whittaker took a seat near the table so that he could have somewhere to rest his notebook if necessary. Brand fitted his cigarette gently into the end of a long ivory holder.

'Mr. Brand, when I last interviewed you and made a reference to 9 Stanton Street you denied all knowledge of the place.'

Brand lighted his cigarette. 'And I still do.'

'I think,' Garth responded, 'you might like to know that one James Mitchell is willing to testify to the fact that he knows you quite well, and that Mr. Dell will shortly be placed under arrest for obstructing the law. He, too, will not have any reason to hold back any information concerning you. It is hardly likely, when they are being hounded by the law, that they will let you escape, is it?'

Brand raised his eyes to watch the smoke curling from his cigarette towards the ceiling.

'Further,' Garth added, 'Miss Hammond swears that you are the same man whom she saw at 9 Stanton Street when you posed as a manservant and sent her away.'

'Clever of her,' Brand sighed. 'Especially when she has never seen me!'

'But she has — in a photograph. I had it taken specially. What is more, I had it touched up so the finished effect was of you standing with a single light shining down on your head and face. Remember when a man bumped into you in Regent Street and knocked your hat off? A van right beside you in the road had photographers inside it . . . They did the rest.'

Brand smiled bitterly. 'You don't imagine that little bit of childish evidence is going to do you any good, do you?'

'Of itself, no — but there are so many other factors. For instance, the evidence will also contain the information given to me by Mr. Dell — namely, that he invited Miss Hammond to 9 Stanton Street, and you wouldn't hear of it. Leslie Carson informed you of Dell's intentions and, for once, you had to abandon your apparent non-connection with Stanton Street and go to the house to stop Dell giving information to Miss Hammond.'

Brand sat down slowly on the chesterfield, a rather cold expression on his swarthy features.

'My apparent non-connection?' he repeated. 'What on earth do you mean by that?'

Garth shrugged. 'Though your money pays the rent for the Stanton Street house — and financed the model of Mr. Dell's invention and his apparent moneyed background — you yourself preferred to remain out of sight, chiefly because your interest was purely a financial return, nothing more. But when you thought the scientific secret of Dell was to be shared with Miss Hammond you stepped in. Even then I don't think you went to the house openly, and I'll tell you why I think you didn't.'

'Kind of you,' Brand murmured. 'I'm most interested.'

'I believe you had made up your mind on a course of action. Once having got to Stanton Street, you were determined to tell Dell that Miss Hammond must not enter that house at any price. How to prevent her? If she got no reply to her knocking she might even try to break in — but you could pretend to be a manservant. In the dim light and the clothes you wear at the salon you could easily get away with it. You could convince her — or try to — that there had been a mistake somewhere on Harvey's part and leave it to him to sort it out with her afterwards. She had never met you as yourself, even though she had heard of you. If later she were to meet you and think you resembled the manservant she saw, you could point to your club alibi as having been there all evening. Later, fortunately for you, that alibi worked out very usefully as an indication of where you were when Hammond was murdered.'

'But I was at the club,' Brand objected. 'Why on earth don't you check up on it?'

Garth's face had relaxed into death-mask immobility.

'I did check on it. You checked in your coat and hat at six-twenty and left again at nine-fifteen. You were seen in the club early in the evening, but nobody could say for certain that you were there *all* the evening. Since you are usually there most evenings your being there that evening was taken for granted by a not over-bright staff. You believed they would swear that you were there. They didn't. When it came to direct questioning they merely assumed so.'

Brand inspected his long cigarette holder pensively.

'There was nothing to stop you leaving by a back window, in just your suit, and getting a taxi to Stanton Street,' Garth added. 'And returning in the same way later on. That is what I think you did do.'

Brand shrugged. 'Anything else?'

'Yes indeed. Once you had managed to convince Miss Hammond that she had made a mistake and sent her away, her father came after her. My guess is that you thought *she* had come back and once again you went to the door. When you found it was Hammond you perhaps tried to send him away — but Hammond was not that kind of man and pushed his way in, as far as the basement. There he saw the equipment which you had been at such pains to prevent his daughter seeing.'

Brand was now watching Garth with a fixed, intent stare as though he were contemplating a particularly dangerous reptile. Whittaker sat scribbling notes in shorthand at the table. A quiet but definite tension gathered in the warm, comfortable room.

'I doubt if by a mere glimpse Hammond could ever have guessed what the equipment was supposed to be,' Garth continued, 'but you, as an unscientific man, could not know that. There is also the possibility that, knowing as you did that Hammond had refused to do a deal with Dell — which made your own investment a dead loss until you found a new backer — you lost your temper in some kind of argument with him and struck him on the head with a wrench . . . I do not say,' Garth finished, 'that you intended to kill him. It was perhaps a blow aimed in impulsive fury more than anything else. The fact remains that the blow *did* kill.'

'Don't you think you'd better be

careful what you say?' Brand asked grimly.

'I've no need to be careful any longer, Mr. Brand. I'm sure of my facts. Why not tell me the truth and make things easier all round?'

'And implicate myself in murder? Do you take me for a damned fool?'

'Hardly — but evidently you seem to think you *deserve* to be called a murderer.'

'Well, all right,' Brant said finally, getting to his feet. 'I admit that I did do those things — pretended to be a manservant, sneaked out of the club, sneaked back, arranged the financial backing for Harvey Dell. But I did not mean to kill Mr. Hammond.'

'You admit, though, that you struck him?'

'Yes.' Brand reflected, examining the cigarette holder again. 'We had an argument. I demanded to know why he hadn't given Harvey Dell a break. Matter of fact I lost my temper and revealed far more than I intended. I realized that I had given everything away about backing

Harvey financially, and that got Hammond into a temper too. Finally I whipped up a wrench, which had been used for the apparatus and hit Hammond on the head. He collapsed, and Carson and I — Carson was down there in the basement with me — found that Hammond was dead.'

'I see.' Garth tightened his lips. 'Then why did you phone Dell later and tell him that Carson hit Hammond?'

Brand hesitated. 'So he told you about that phone call, did he?'

'He told me quite a deal, and I'm repeating the question. Why did you shift the blame to Carson?'

Brand did not answer. He seemed to be thinking hard.

'I'll tell you why,' Garth said, a glint in his eyes. 'It was because, when you made that phone call, Carson was dead. Because that was so, you knew that he would never be able to deny but what he had killed Hammond. Dead men can't defend themselves. Don't interrupt me!' Garth insisted, as Brand half started to speak. 'You have said that Carson was down there in the basement with you, a conclusion at which I had already arrived. There is not much doubt in my mind but what Carson was an honest — too honest — sort of chap. The very fact that he agreed to Dell showing Miss Hammond the invention pointed to a pretty generous type of nature and not one concerned only with personal gain. Never expecting the way you would take it he even came and told you . . . He was then a witness to your striking, and killing, Hammond. He was not the type of man to keep quiet about it, either. You had only one alternative — to strangle him. And a big man like you would have had no difficulty in doing it.'

'I notice,' Brand snapped, 'that you leave Harvey Dell out of this! How do you know where he was, what he was doing? Where is your proof that I did such a thing to Carson?'

Garth said: 'You have admitted striking and killing Hammond. All right: that I had guessed, chiefly because Carson had no motive for wanting to be rid of Hammond, but you had — the loss of your investment. Dell is in the clear because I have definitely proved that on the night in question he was halfway between Lancing and London, and unable to influence events in either place. Further, he would never have killed Hammond, the father of the girl he loves. I came to that conclusion long ago.'

'Loves?' Brand repeated. 'The whole thing was a business arrangement!'

'Originally,' Garth agreed. 'Nature sometimes has the last say, though . . . When I questioned Mr. Dell about you he said that you would never have murdered Carson because he — Carson — was 'the goose which laid the golden eggs'. Since I was sure nobody else could have done it I realized that necessity had compelled you to murder him. In other words, he had been a witness to the death of Hammond — and possibly to his disappearance as well. You had everything handy — a boat at the base of the shaft, a ladder to climb down. All you had to do was dismantle all the apparatus and throw it down the shaft, then upset and sink the generator in the stream. The thing that did puzzle me was how an unscientific man like you would know what vital parts to remove . . .

'Then I hit on a possible answer. That something incredible had happened in regard to Hammond — so incredible that Carson, alive at that time, insisted that you both leave immediately and make the place look as though it had never been used. So it was probably Carson who removed the vital parts and kept them, and you took them from his dead body when, in the boat, you killed him. Since his body was found in the Thames you evidently tipped him out into the river after strangling him.'

'You sound mighty hazy about what happened to Hammond,' Brand commented sourly.

'I am,' Garth admitted. 'And I shall continue to be so until a scientific specialist finds the right answer . . . ' He got to his feet. 'In the meantime, Clifton Brand, I must ask you to accompany me to headquarters. There you will be formally charged with the murder of Benson Thomas Hammond and Leslie

Carson and be placed in custody . . . You're not obliged to say anything in answer to the charge unless you wish to do so, but whatever you say will be taken down in writing and may be used in evidence.'

'I know, I know . . . ' Brand crushed his cigarette in the ashtray and put the holder in the breast pocket of his gown. 'All right, I'll come without trouble . . . Look here, how much easier will it make it if I say something? Explain what really happened?'

Garth shrugged. 'It's not for me to say. I've cautioned you about saying anything: if you wish to make a voluntary statement you can do so. It will not be for me to cross-examine you unless it's to render some doubtful point clearer.'

'All right then — it's about Hammond. After I found he was dead I had to do some swift thinking. I was all for throwing his body into the stream below, then it occurred to me that at an experiment I had seen that apparatus of Harvey Dell's do some mighty queer things. It makes things vanish, you know.'

Garth's face was expressionless. 'So?'

'I pushed Hammond's body into the magnet-thing. I asked Carson if that was the right place to put it to make it vanish. He seemed to only half grasp what I was up to and I slammed the main switch. Hammond . . . just disappeared. You can believe it or not!'

Brand passed a hand quickly over his forehead.

'I felt better then,' he said. 'I was convinced that his body had somehow been utterly destroyed and that nobody would know what had happened to it. Carson said that he didn't agree with me and went into some high-flown technical explanation as to why the body would appear somewhere else. I had no time to argue about such things and told him that, since a chauffeur was waiting outside and Hammond was known to have entered the house, we had got to *do* something.

'He agreed with me and took the apparatus to bits in record time. It was made in sections. He kept some parts and threw the rest down the shaft. Then we took down all the portable stuff — curtains, lamps, and so on. Carson explained that it was all movable in case anybody undesirable tried to enter the house some time and it became necessary to decamp — '

'So you removed everything,' Garth interrupted. 'And even laid dust. Then what?'

'Carson laid the dust with a bellows-thing.' Brand was breathing hard. 'Then we started off in a rowboat down the stream, and on the way Carson sat thinking — He was, he said, pretty sure that we hadn't got rid of Hammond's body at all, that it would turn up in Lancing. I asked him why and he said that the apparatus had been tuned ready for just that purpose when Miss Hammond was expected. I couldn't make head nor tail of what he meant.'

'But surely you knew in what kind of an invention you had sunk your money?' Garth asked in surprise.

'All I knew about it was that it could cut down distances for freight lines. I didn't question it overmuch for two reasons. I don't understand science, and don't want to — and for another, I was prepared to believe anything of Harvey's because I know his scientific brilliance . . . Carson said that if the body did turn up he'd be bound, in his own interests, to say what had happened. That meant that I would be accused of murder and that the secret of the invention would be a secret no longer. As things stood then, I felt that Harvey and I, and Jimmy Mitchell, our distant partner, still had a chance to clean up with somebody else . . . so I silenced Carson. I had no other course that I could see. It wasn't revenge,' Brand added anxiously. 'It wasn't cold-blooded murder, or anything like that. I just had to, to protect my own interests and Harvey's.'

'Murder,' Garth said, 'is murder. You can't dress it up.'

'Well, I've told you what happened, and that's the truth. I telephoned Harvey and told him what had occurred — but to make myself safe I told him that Carson had killed Hammond, which made Carson's disappearance seem logical. I thought he would drift out to sea and never be found — but evidently I guessed wrong. The next thing I heard was that Hammond's body had turned up, so Harvey and I agreed to keep separated as much as possible because he wanted to give Carson, whom he still thought the guilty one, a chance to explain himself.'

'Why?' Garth asked.

'Harvey Dell had the idea that Carson had committed murder accidentally because Mr. Hammond suffered from some kind of disease which made his bones soft, therefore a mere tap from Carson had killed him. Harvey Dell wanted to give Carson a chance to give himself up and explain. When he heard that his body had been found I don't know what he thought.'

'I can tell you,' Garth responded. 'He knew then that only you could have done it, but for the sake of his invention he still kept quiet. The incident did, however, make him less resolute about it and he made what was practically a full confession to me — except for the details of his invention.'

Brand said nothing. He started slightly

as the coal in the fire slipped inwards in a cloud of sparks.

'We'd better be on our way,' Garth said. 'Sergeant, go upstairs with Mr. Brand whilst he dresses.'

16

Upon his return to his office after dealing with the charge against Clifton Brand, Garth found a memo awaiting him. It said briefly — *Ring up Grimshaw, Worthing Police*.

'If this is what I think it is,' Garth said, picking up the telephone, 'we've about roped in all the lads in this business.'

'Garth here,' the chief inspector said presently. 'What news, Grimshaw?'

'I've got Dell and Mitchell under lock and key, as you ordered. I charged them with obstruction. We kept a watch on the main London-Brighton road and when Dell's car appeared we followed it. He was also being followed by a patrol car from London. He didn't go to the hut: instead he went to see Mitchell at his rooms in Lancing. We waited until he came out — with Mitchell — and I questioned them.'

'Then?'

'They were evasive, but I got the impression that they were going to the hut together to make trouble. So I took both of 'em in charge.'

'Okay. Best thing you can do is drive the pair of them over here; I want to talk to them. The real villain is Clifton Brand, and I've charged him with murder. All Dell and Mitchell have done is commit misdemeanors but they'll have to answer for them, of course . . . What about Dr. Carruthers? What's he doing?'

'He left the hut not twenty minutes ago and said he would get in touch with you personally. He said he was taking the train home. I had a constable drive him to the station.'

'All right, Grimshaw, thanks,' Garth responded. 'You'd better come with Dell and Mitchell yourself: I'd like to have a few words with you just to get the final details straight. Leave a guard on that hut.'

Garth hung up and glanced at Whittaker as he frowned. 'Doesn't seem to be much you can do to Mitchell and Dell sir,' he remarked. 'They're not guilty of felony,

331

nor are they principals in the second degree: they didn't actively aid Brand in his dirty work. They're not accessories before or after the fact, so — '

'Forget the book of Common Law, man!' Garth growled. 'My arresting them is just a token act. As a man I'm sorry for them and the mess they've got into: as a police officer I have got to enforce the law. They've obstructed justice, and that is the only indictable offence with which I can charge them. In any case there's no reason why the magistrate should not grant bail.'

'And what about Miss Barrow, sir?'

Garth smiled sourly. 'Her threats didn't even hint at murder: they were just plain silly — 'Any moment now'. 'Your hour is coming' . . . I'm not interested in Miss Barrow. We have Clifton Brand, and that's the main thing. As for Harvey Dell, I think Miss Hammond had better know the circumstances. If bail is allowed she is the one to provide it, I imagine. Then we can — ' The telephone rang.

'Garth here. Yes?'

Pause — then an irate, high-pitched

voice, unmistakably that of Dr. Carruthers, came over the line.

'You'd better get over to my place first thing in the morning, Garth — nine o'clock sharp. I've worked everything out, and I'll show you the whole thing tomorrow. You'd better come in your car because we'll be taking a trip to Lancing tomorrow morning. I've asked Gordon — my male secretary — to give me a hand. I'll explain everything in the morning. 'Bye.'

The line clicked and Garth put the telephone down. Whittaker, who had overheard, nodded. 'Just a matter of waiting and seeing, sir — I'd better get Brand's statement typed out, hadn't I?'

'Uh-huh. I'm not going home until Grimshaw has brought in Dell and Mitchell — Which reminds me, I'd better have a word with Miss Hammond.'

★　★　★

It was nine o'clock the following morning when Whittaker pulled up the police car outside Carruthers's home. Mrs. Barret admitted the sergeant and Garth and motioned them towards the door at the side of the staircase. They found Carruthers silently contemplating the queer horseshoe-shaped apparatus, which they had seen on the previous occasion.

'Glad you're punctual for a change,' he commented, glancing up.

Garth looked at the apparatus. 'Anything going to happen?' he inquired.

'Everything, I hope. I'm waiting for a phone call from Gordon: he's working at the Lancing end. I suppose the young fathead's slept late, or something. I said nine o'clock.'

'You mean he's phoning from Lancing?'

'Yes. You see, I have to give him instructions. Can't be dashing up and down myself: it would take too long.' Carruthers grinned. 'In fact I don't think Gordon is particularly pleased with this sudden assignment. He had to leave his wife in London and find himself an hotel in Worthing at a moment's notice. One of the trials of being assistant to the 'Admirable Crichton' of science.'

Just then the telephone rang. Carruthers

picked it up and Garth and Whittaker stood listening to the one-sided conversation.

' 'Bout time you showed up, Gordon . . . Look, here's what I want. Set that direction-indicator on four-five-seven and close switches seven and eight. Then you'll have to pay out those two cable drums and clip two leads on to the overhead lines. Get the police to help you — Yes. When you've done that, ring me back. 'Bye.'

Garth said: 'He's taking a risk shinning up a power-pylon to anchor his leads on to ten thousand volts, isn't he?'

'Not really,' the physicist replied. 'Anyway, Mitchell took that risk every time — *and* the risk of being caught, too. I imagine the powerhouse engineers must have wondered now and again at the sudden extra load on their power — By the way, Garth, what's been happening at your end? Was my idea about Mitchell giving himself away correct?'

'Er — yes,' the chief inspector admitted. 'He spoke to Harvey Dell, and Dell went chasing after him. I had the pair of them arrested for misdemeanor. They were charged last night and then released on bail. Miss Hammond tipped up the money.'

'Whatever happens, Garth, don't fool about with the law in trying to make Harvey Dell smart. Men like him are all too rare in the scientific world today. To put him in clink for several years would set the profession back a decade. As to Mitchell, I don't think he counts for much. Leslie Carson was another like Dell — an electrical genius. It's a thousand pities that Brand had to murder him.'

Garth gave a start. 'I didn't say he did,' he commented. 'Who told you?'

'Nobody,' Carruthers responded insolently. 'It couldn't be anybody else but Brand. If you haven't arrested him yet, you should.'

'I have . . . As to Dell, he won't get a heavy sentence, or Mitchell either. Misdemeanors sometimes don't even carry a conviction. I'll do all I can to get his release because it is perfectly obvious that his silence was chiefly on account of his fear that the invention would slip out of his hands.'

Carruthers nodded slowly and turned to the bench. From it he lifted the teapot with a knitted cosy. He raised the lid of the pot and looked into it. Then he held it forward.

'Take a look,' he ordered.

Garth looked. 'So it has tea in it,' he said. 'What about it?'

'You'll see. Confound Gordon! How the blazes much longer is he going to be, I wonder? Here, Garth — mark your initials on the lid of this teapot.'

Garth hesitated, frowned, then tugged out his penknife and snapped open the blade. With the point of it he scratched 'M.G.' in the aluminium.

'Thanks,' Carruthers acknowledged, looking at it — and he took the teapot, still with the cosy about it, towards the queerly designed apparatus. Almost reverently he laid the teapot on the metal plating immediately within the area of the horseshoe magnet. He said nothing, but waited through an interval — then he jumped into action as the telephone rang.

'Yes?' he said curtly into the transmitter.

'You have? Good! All right — close number one switch and that will set the dynamos working from the power lines. After that stand back in case there is some kind of explosion. I don't think there will be, but a big displacement of air is possible . . . I'll wait two minutes to give you time to get all set.'

Carruthers rang off and grinned half to himself. Then he rubbed his hands gently together and looked at the teapot — a prosaic, uninteresting object in the area of the magnet.

Garth asked a question: 'How you suppose that Harvey Dell, or Carson, kept in touch with Mitchell when conducting his experiments in the Stanton Street basement?'

'I don't think a telephone was used at all for Mitchell and Dell — or Carson — to exchange notes,' Carruthers responded 'They could have used short-wave radio. Probably they used code words so that anybody else picking them up would merely think they were ham radio enthusiasts at work. Certainly they must have communicated somehow in order to be sure that their instruments worked in unison.'

Carruthers waited a few moments longer, looked at the electric clock on the wall, and then went over to a switch-panel.

'Watch carefully, gentlemen,' he instructed, and slammed home the master-switch of the apparatus amidst a transient flaring of blue sparks.

The mysterious instrumentation that made up the main body of the equipment glowed warm lavender and there was a humming of power. A sense of tremendous electrical strain surged through the air and made the hairs on the back of Garth and Whittaker's necks bristle. Then came a peculiar aroma.

'Ozone!' Whittaker exclaimed. 'We could smell that when we entered that house in Stanton Street for the first time.'

'Yes, ozone,' Carruthers agreed. 'Three atoms to ozone instead of two to the normal oxygen, produced by electrical reaction — same as a thunderstorm sometimes produces . . . However, observe!'

Garth and Whittaker did not need the

instruction. Before their eyes the teapot inside its woolen cosy was mysteriously becoming transparent, until finally it vanished altogether and the metal plate was empty.

Carruthers switched off the apparatus and motioned towards the staircase. 'Next stop Lancing,' he announced. 'Come on.'

Garth and Whittaker followed him quickly, waiting only long enough for him to scramble into his enormous overcoat. Then with the tails flying the little physicist led the way out to the police car.

Whittaker sped the car down the quiet, suburban avenue, turned right into the Halingford main road, and then opened up. Garth, brooding in the back of the car, presently turned his pale eyes on the scientist.

'I suppose, Doctor, that it would break your heart to explain how that trick with the teapot was done?'

Carruthers grinned. 'I must have absolute proof that I've been successful before I'll say anything. That proof can only be at Lancing — in the shape of a teapot with tea inside it.' Garth gave a disbelieving smile and fished for his cheroot case.

'You don't believe it?' Carruthers asked cynically. 'Well, I can't say I blame you. Nobody believed Edison, or Alexander Bell, or Lister, and sometimes people do not believe Hiram J. Carruthers. In the end they are compelled to by the march of events. Remember that I told you Harvey Dell is a genius — a century ahead of his time.'

'If that fantastic apparatus of his can transfer a teapot — with tea in it — for sixty miles, then I'll agree that he is a genius,' Garth said.

The journey over, Whittaker pulled up at length on the road on a line with Mitchell's hut perched on the rising downland. Outside it were two constables on guard. They watched the party advancing and then stood aside at the sight of Garth's warrant card.

'My assistant in there?' Carruthers asked briefly.

'Yes, sir. Waiting for you, I think.'

The constable opened the hut door and Carruthers stepped inside with Whittaker and Garth behind him. A tall young man with curly black hair and grey eyes, his handsome features marred by a sickle-shaped scar down the right cheek, got to his feet from the solitary chair. He gave a welcoming smile.

'Hallo there, Doc. Glad you got here. 'Morning,' he added, as Carruthers identified Garth and Whittaker.

'My assistant, Gordon Drew,' Carruthers explained; and then he looked about him. 'Well, Gordon, what happened?'

'Everything! I got the shock of my life when a teapot appeared under the magnet.'

'Was there much air displacement?'

'Not much,' Drew responded. 'Just a flash that seemed to come from nowhere, and then the teapot materialized. Soon as I saw that, I knew who was back of the experiment,' Drew added, grinning. He turned to the bench beside him and handed the teapot over. Carruthers took it and examined it.

'Hmmm. Just as I expected. Here, Garth, take a look at it.'

Looking like a man who has witnessed

an extremely baffling conjuring trick, Garth took the teapot and peered at the hinged lid. His initials were still there, exactly as he had made them.

'I'll be damned!' he declared frankly, and opening the lid he looked inside. 'And tea still in it! Congratulations, Doctor!'

'Don't congratulate me; congratulate Dell. He thought of the idea. But,' Carruthers added, 'there is something wrong. Notice?'

Garth contemplated the teapot again, frowning, his cheroot jutting. Whittaker looked with him and finally gave an exclamation.

'Yes, there is!' he cried. 'The spout is where the handle should be, and the handle's where the spout should be! The hinge is over the spout instead of the handle. That's all wrong. And — and the cosy-cover is inside out! Those lines of knitting have knots in them.'

'Exactly.' Carruthers looked pleased; then he glanced at Drew. 'You haven't touched the pot at all, beyond lifting it from the receiving plate, have you?'

'Be more than my life's worth,' Gordon Drew responded gravely.

'Then,' the physicist said, 'that means there is a defect. And that same defect transferred Mr. Hammond's internal organs and broke all his bones — or rather did not allow them to recast in their original form.'

Garth put the teapot back on the bench and then looked at Carruthers questioningly.

'Look here, Doctor, don't you think it's time you stopped playing around and told us what this is all about? What is this confounded invention?'

'It is a matter-transferrer,' Carruthers responded. He half sat on the bench, swinging his short little legs. 'Putting it in plain language — this instrument broadcasts solids. I've hunted for this idea throughout my scientific career,' Carruthers continued, 'because I have known it to be possible — but I never seemed to quite get it. Dell has gone ahead and done it, only it still isn't perfect. There's a fault in his patterner somewhere.'

'His what?' Garth asked hazily.

'The patterner.' Carruthers sighed. 'Sound and vision can be — and are — transmitted by radio waves. Right?'

'Certainly. Radio and television.'

'Very well then. Odours can also be transmitted over short distances by the American Electronic Laboratory. From sound vision, and odour, it is only one step further to solids . . . And that is what Harvey Dell has accomplished. His apparatus behaves exactly as a radio transmitter does, only it incorporates a different and much more complex circuit. By electronic vibration a solid is broken down in the electric field of the instrument into its exact number of atomic groups, just the same as sound is transformed into electrons and then reformed at the receiving end. Once the atomic set-up is complete it comprises a very small mass since even the biggest solid is mainly composed of space. It becomes, technically, an atom-pack . . . '

Garth was groping. 'You — you mean the sort of essence of the whole thing? All the original ingredients are there, compressed, and in the form of energy instead of the visible, solid outline?'

'Good! You have it!' Carruthers approved. 'After that the energy is absorbed into the magnet and passed through the transformers and transmitter. It is then broadcast on a normal radio beam. At the other end of that beam is the receiver — this apparatus here. It simply works in the reverse of the transmitter and reforms whatever it has received. More plainly, whatever is transmitted from the other end reappears here, just as a radio set reforms whatever a studio is sending out in sound or vision.'

'And that . . . is what happened to Hammond?' Garth demanded.

'Obviously. Brand pushed him in the apparatus and closed the switches. Hammond was transferred to here where the receiver stands. The transmitter beam must have been tuned upon it at the time. Hammond reappeared and Mitchell must have been present when that happened. But in the process Hammond got 'scrambled up', so to speak. His bones did not reform in the original pattern and his internal organs were misplaced. That alone would have killed him had he not been dead, but as it happened he was a corpse anyway. The whole thing would be accomplished in less than a second since radio waves move at the speed of light.'

'Seems unbelievable,' Garth muttered.

'Not a bit of it.' Carruthers slapped a palm emphatically on the bench. 'Get this into your head, Garth! A solid — and that includes liquids, of course; in fact it includes everything except a gas — is composed of certain known atomic patterns. It is no more difficult to transfer it in its entirety as it is to transfer every feature of a face or every intonation of a voice . . . '

'So that explains what Dell meant when he talked of freight and cutting down distances,' Garth mused. 'Evidently his idea was to interest Hammond in the scheme because, had Hammond taken over the rights in it, he would have been able to transfer anything to any part of the world where there were receivers.'

'Just so: bigger receivers for bigger

objects. No limit to the size with transmitters and receivers big enough. To my mind, two million was a modest estimate for the terrific scope of the plan.'

'It still seems unbelievable,' Garth declared.

Carruthers grinned. 'You are descended, my earthbound friend from the hecklers who shouted down Pasteur. At the beginning of the Second World War nobody thought of radar or flying bombs outside the realm of stories — but they happened. Transmittal of solids is only on the natural path of science and Harvey Dell's name will go down in scientific history amongst the illustrious.'

'No wonder he went to any length to preserve the secret.' Whittaker commented.

Garth stirred. 'In all my career I've never come up against anything like this — and until I get the full details the A C. is liable to have me certified, or something. Whitty, call the Yard. Tell them to get hold of Harvey Dell again and have him come to my office in time for when I get back — say about three this afternoon. We'll have lunch, and then I'm going to have a few words with Mitchell before we carry on to London.'

*   *   *

Immediately after lunch Garth made his call on the Government-controlled farm and found Mitchell at work as usual — until his bail expired. The laboratory superintendent indicated the door of a private room as Garth, Whittaker, and Caruthers stood looking about them.

Presently Mitchell came in to them, his expression grim. 'What am I supposed to have done now?'

'If you have any sense, Mr. Mitchell, you haven't done anything further,' Garth responded. 'I'm here to ask you a few questions — and there is no point in you holding out any more. Dr. Carruthers will tell you just how much we know.'

The little physicist did so in his blunt, half-quarrelsome fashion. When he had finished Mitchell sighed. 'Which is about the whole story,' he admitted. 'Though I hardly understand the mechanics myself.'

'Never mind the mechanics,' Garth

said. 'Just where did you fit into the scheme? You were in it from the start, weren't you?'

'I had charge of the receiving end, as Harvey's friend. That is why that hut was bought, with Brand's money.'

'And you're not really a 'ham' radio enthusiast?' Carruthers asked.

'No; that was just a cover-up suggested by Harvey to disguise my real activities. The only 'hamming' I did was between the hut and the basement in London, on shortwave radio.'

Carruthers gave a satisfied grin.

'Radio equipment being what it is,' Mitchell added, 'I guessed that even if anybody saw it they'd never know its real purpose. Only a man like you, Dr. Carruthers, would be able to tell its real significance.'

'Naturally,' the physicist assented calmly.

'Did you know that Hammond's body was going to be sent?' Garth asked.

'No, I didn't.' Mitchell didn't hesitate. 'About half an hour before Hammond's body appeared in the receiver I had received a short-wave call from Harvey.

He told me to have the apparatus working and ready to receive some kind of object. He did not stipulate what it would be. So I followed out orders and waited. When *Hammond* turned up, mysteriously boneless I was panic-stricken. I couldn't imagine what had gone wrong at the transmitting end. I knew him from his photograph, and naturally I knew that Harvey was hoping to become engaged to his daughter. I did the only thing I could think of — carried his body to the road, and some job it was! I left it there in the hope that the very mystery of his arrival and his smashed bones would make the police think a hit-and-run was responsible.'

'Which accounted for your one heavy set of footprints?' Garth asked.

'Yes. There were three sets of prints that were light, when I went back and forth to the hut, and the final set was heavy from when I carried Hammond. That heavy equipment gag, which I mentioned to the police, was purely an inspiration. I have a heavy old panel on my car, and I used it for an alibi.'

'Then what happened?'

'I got a phone call to my rooms from Harvey, telling me to remove as much of the important apparatus as I could. He asked me all about what had occurred and then told me that he believed Carson was responsible. I was to keep quiet . . . He also said that after his quarrel with Brand he went for a drive and headed towards Lancing, because it had occurred to him that all this time I must be waiting by the receiver for whatever he was going to send. He couldn't get in touch with me at the hut, so he went back to London, satisfied that I'd conclude something had gone wrong. In the interval Hammond was transmitted . . . Harvey rang me up at my rooms the moment he knew of it.'

Garth reflected. 'Then what did you do?'

'That night I returned to my hut circuitously and left only the four original footprint trails. I'd have moved those too only I thought that would be overdoing it, because I must have had some way of getting to the hut.'

'Which,' the chief inspector said,

getting to his feet, 'is all I need to know. Thank you, Mr. Mitchell. I'll do what I can to help you and Mr. Dell. I'm satisfied that both of you were innocent parties in the whole thing.'

'That's good hearing, Inspector! And what about Harvey? Will his invention be — '

'If you were going to say 'confiscated', it will not!' Carruthers declared. 'I, personally, will see to that. In fact I'll do more: I'll make the Cavendish Laboratory find the right financial backing and buy shares in the Company which will be bound to follow. When I talk, scientists listen.'

'I think we're all done here,' Garth commented. 'Come on — let's be getting back to London and have Dell clear up the last details.'